Dreams Like Thunder

DREAMS LIKE THUNDER

DIANE SIMMONS

STORY LINE PRESS
1995

Second American Printing

This publication was made possible thanks in part to the generous support of the Andrew W. Mellon Foundation and our individual contributors.

ISBN: 0-934257-64-7 (cloth)
ISBN: 1-885266-03-0 (paper)

Published by Story Line Press
Three Oaks Farm
Brownsville, OR
97327-9718

Interior design by Lysa McDowell
Paperback cover design by Chiquita Babb

ACKNOWLEDGEMENTS

Portions of this book were originally published in the following publications: *Fiction, Whetstone, Northwest Review,* and *North Country.*

Special thanks to the MacDowell Colony, the City College of New York Graduate Writing Program, and the Cummington Community of the Arts.

TABLE OF CONTENTS

In memory of Vina Gover Ellis, 1898–1990,
and W. Dale Ellis, 1919–1989.

For Burt, and Jane

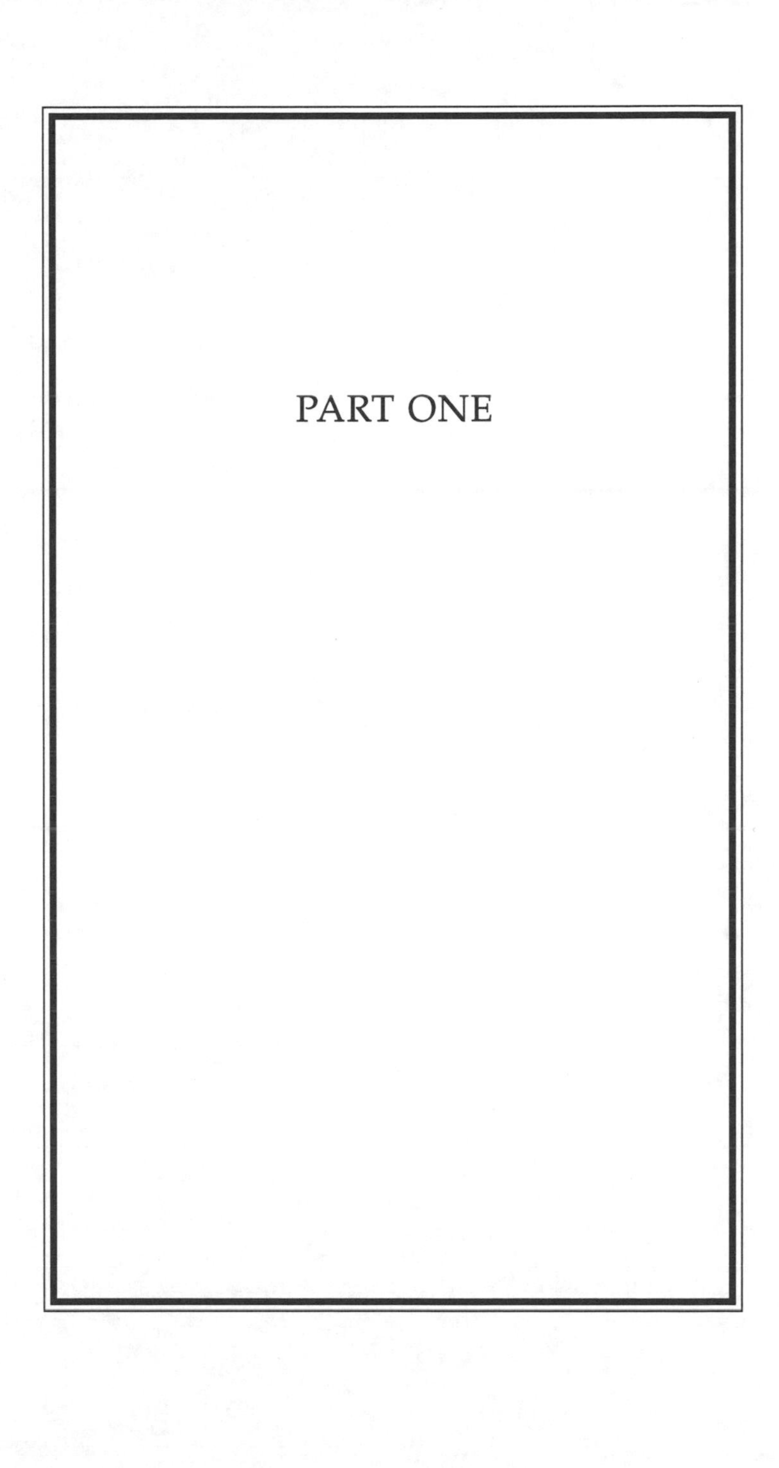

PART ONE

Every day during haying Grandma came around from her house and looked in at them through the screen door. After a minute she would come inside and stand watching them, her arms crossed tight over her chest. She was stringy and tough with hard black eyes and sometimes she looked like a little old Indian chief. She came every day after dinner to see Mama and Alberta in the hot greasy kitchen, the wind knocked out of their sails.

"Did they get the hay chopper fixed?" she would ask. Or, "Will they be finished with the upper field tonight, do they think?"

The farm, the two houses, the barn, everything belonged to Grandma. Dad only worked it for her. So they had to answer all her questions, Alberta speaking if possible to spare Mama.

Mama, in one light, was just a visitor. Whereas Alberta, after Dad, was the only heir. So Alberta stared right back at Grandma and didn't take any guff.

Mama hardly ever spoke to Grandma. Not when Grandma would rearrange Mama's wash on the clothesline or when she came in and changed the heat under pots that were cooking. There was only the one windy morning when Grandma built a leaf fire right after Mama hung out a wash. Mama saw the fire from the kitchen window and saw the smoke blowing on the clean clothes. Still she didn't speak, but took off her apron and went up over the cellar to get her trunks to pack and leave.

At first it seemed funny but Mama kept packing all day and it became possible that she could somehow get back to Alabama and to her aunts and maids. Then she could forget she had ever married and come out west to a farm.

"You better stop her," Alberta told Dad when he came in from irrigating.

But the next morning Mama left on the mail stage to

Bonner, forty-two miles up the river. From there she could get the Greyhound to Alabama.

After she left, Grandma and Dad met out in the barnyard so they could talk out of earshot. Alberta, watching from the house, saw Grandma talk, her arms folded, her skirt whipping in the wind. Once Dad threw down his hat and stomped on it. Then he picked it up and brushed it off.

"You better go bring her back," Alberta told Dad when he came in. Then she said it again because they could not let her leave, even if she wanted to. So he drove to Bonner where Mama was waiting for the bus at the Geyser Grand Hotel and got her to come back.

After that nothing changed, or maybe it even made Grandma stronger.

On this day Grandma only came in briefly, to hear that haying was going fine and to tell Alberta there were lots of potato bugs she could kill if she wanted to earn money at a penny per five dead bugs.

Then she left and they hurried with their work, watching now for the mail car to come down the road, hoping for one of the Christmas catalogs that started coming usually in August but might come in late July. Other than that there wasn't much to hope for in the mail. Once Alberta had had a pen pal in Wales and you never knew when a thin blue letter might come. At first the girl in Wales seemed especially interested in writing to Alberta since the steps to her house in Wales were made from Oregon pine. Alberta had written back, falsely, that there was Oregon pine growing all around, even in their yard. In truth there were pine trees up in the hills, but here in the valley there were only leafy trees that people had planted when they first came from Kentucky. Between the irrigated floor of the valley and the mountains there were no trees at all, just the dry foothills where nothing grew but sagebrush.

After that, the girl in Wales had never written another letter, though Alberta had written several times more, asking all about Wales and not mentioning Oregon pine.

But this day, when the kitchen was finally clean and Alberta could go out to the mail box, there was a blue foreign letter addressed to Mama who came out in the front yard to read it. It was from one of her aunts who was in Japan with her husband, a colonel in the Army. Mama sat under the big silver-leaf tree that shaded the whole yard. She read the letter, then said, "They are coming here on their way home from Japan."

"How will they get here from Japan?"

"They'll fly to Bonner. We'll have to go pick them up."

They sat for a while under the big tree. Their old dog Mike came to jump on them and Alberta held him off while Mama read the letter once more. It was an aunt Mama hadn't seen for years and years, since the war when they both married somebody in the service. The aunt had gotten to Japan because of the war, like Mama had gotten to Oregon.

The colonel wasn't coming. It was just Aunt Rae and Martha Lee, a cousin Alberta had never met and barely heard of.

"Martha Lee just is quite accomplished," Mama read from Aunt Rae's letter, her Southern accent seeming to increase as she spoke Aunt Rae's words. "She plays the violin and is the one who speaks Japanese and translates for us."

They sat under the silver-leaf tree in the afternoon heat, the clatter and roar of the hay chopper just barely drifting up from the field. Alberta pictured Martha Lee giving a violin concert for the hay men in the back yard. The hay men had their hats off so you could see their white foreheads where the sun never hit. They clapped and whistled when she finished playing, but Martha Lee only dipped her head meekly and spoke some soft Japanese so that the hay men were amazed.

Alberta played no musical instrument and had only

recently started taking baton twirling lessons from the coach's wife. But she was heir to the farm and all the buildings, and so stood a little ways off, her arms crossed, watching Martha Lee perform, not having to worry much.

"We'll have to wash all the crystal," Mama said. "And all the china. We'll have a reception."

Alberta waited to hear what else they would do, but Mama went to sunbathe like she did every day after dinner, back behind the chicken house where Grandma couldn't see. She kept a plastic lounge chair out there and came out from the house tiptoeing in her bathing suit, carrying a towel and two little circles of tin foil the size of quarters.

She lay down on the lounge chair and fixed a circle of tin foil over each of her eyes. She didn't like to talk while she sunbathed but Alberta went along anyway, sitting on the ground, petting old Mike's blue neck and looking at Mama who was lying there blind. Alberta studied her as a person from Alabama, to get ready a little for the people coming.

Sometimes Mama seemed too fat. Her bottom seemed too wide and even lying down with two layers of tight bathing suit holding it in, her stomach wasn't flat. Sometimes her nose seemed too big, better if it were small and pointed up at the end. Yet, as Alberta studied the things wrong, she knew Mama was beautiful anyway. You could tell it by the way the hay men at the dinner table blushed when she spoke to them. You could tell most by the way she looked at herself in the mirror trying on clothes, her chin high, her eyes nearly shut.

Even now in the baking sun, Mama's soft tanned skin seemed to glow, containing secrets none of them from Oregon would ever know and would only see the faintest light of escaping. They were secrets of Alabama, the maids and the aunts back there. Was she dreaming even now with the tin foil reflecting her eyes back inside to some Alabama scene? Did she hear her aunts with their high pitched Southern yells, and was she eating refreshments from a tray brought by a maid? And if she was, was it true? Or was it a made-up Alabama Mama saw, now that she had come so far away?

Possibly Aunt Rae was coming to help Mama escape back to Alabama.

"Maybe you could go back with Aunt Rae when she goes," Alberta said in a kidding tone.

Mama though didn't answer, probably asleep, her tin-foiled eyes aimed right at the sun.

Grandma too went into kind of a state after dinner, napping, but still sitting up at her table with her dinner dishes around. If you looked carefully, you could see the shiny brown crumbs of the store-bought chocolate cupcakes which came two to a cellophane package and had whipped cream inside. Grandma secretly ate one every day for dessert unless someone was there. She bought them secretly and hid them in the tablecloth drawer but they all knew she had one every day.

Grandma didn't admit she ate the cupcakes and then she didn't admit she napped after dinner so Alberta would sneak up on her to prove she did. Alberta would go in silently through the back screen door, creep through the kitchen, then crouch for a long time right by Grandma's elbow, watching her doze over her plate, her arms crossed on her chest, the *Reader's Digest* propped on the sugar bowl as if she were reading. While she dozed, she frowned, like she did during prayers at church, and held her fists tight. Alberta looked at how skinny her arms and hands were and how the big blue veins seemed to run all over her body, tying her up into a tight package.

Grandma had been born in the valley and her papa, Thomas Pratt, had been one of the first white people here. He had come on horseback from Kentucky and ended up with a big spread and a fine house.

Then, mysteriously, they had lost most of their land, all but the home place. The fine house Thomas Pratt built burned down while Grandma was still a girl and that was probably what made her so jumpy.

Now, after sitting and watching for a long time, Alberta yelled "Boo!" and Grandma jerked awake.

"Dickens," she said. "Do that again and I'll paddle you."

But Alberta was the one person Grandma couldn't scare.

She got up to do her dishes and Alberta went to sit on top of the kitchen counter, leaning out the window and smelling the hard smell of Grandma's geraniums.

"I trust they aren't coming next week," Grandma said when she heard about the company.

"Because," Grandma said, "Uncle Edmund will be here next week."

This was Grandma's older brother who they heard had gotten married again though he was about seventy-five.

"He won't stay overnight with us even if he does come," Alberta said. "He never stays more than an hour."

"He might well stay," Grandma said. "He used to stay."

But he hadn't stayed since one Memorial Day weekend long ago when Grandma had put the dishes he ate off in the bathtub with disinfectant.

Grandma slammed her dishes around in the dish pan, mad about something she wasn't ready to mention yet.

"Well," Alberta said. "There's still room for Aunt Rae and Martha Lee even if he does stay because they can have my room and I'll sleep in a tent."

She did not believe Grandma would really try to stop people coming from Japan, but she got tired of how Grandma was against everything that came from away. She got down from the counter to leave. She'd thought Grandma would like to hear some news, but now she wished she hadn't told. She wished they could have just come, smelling different in hats and shiny shoes with heavy blond suitcases stacked all around like people you saw at the Greyhound Station. And Grandma would have finally come out her back door, humming, secretly trying to see who had come. She would come strolling through the back yard like, "dum-de-dum, I'm just trying to find my hoe," and when she saw Alberta she would grab her and say, "Who's that drove up?" And Alberta would say, "Oh, just Martha Lee, my cousin from Japan." Then Grandma would be furious at nobody telling her. Her eyes would go black and hard as rocks and she would go out by the ditch and look for water snakes to whack in two.

"The reason I put Edmund's dishes in disinfectant," Grandma said, "is that he was living in The Dalles where they have that TB sanitarium. And Edmund would never be careful."

Alberta went out anyway, letting the screen door bam. From the field you could hear the racket of the hay chopper and of the lumbering old trucks that followed along behind to catch the hay. She had just about decided to go down to ride in the truck with Hank Hopper, the hay man with the black Buick and the duck-tailed haircut. But inside the house, Grandma's hard heels started to clickety-click on the kitchen floor and dishes began crashing together. Alberta went back in to see Grandma scooping everything off the table into a dish pan, even the sugar bowl and the salt shaker.

"It's Edmund and her," Grandma said. "Oh, why doesn't he say when he's coming a week early. Straighten those chairs." She shoved the pan of dishes under the sink, knocking the soaps and bleaches back out of the way. "Swipe those crumbs off," she told Alberta. "Smooth the cloth."

Alberta brushed the crumbs off the white table cloth and onto the floor, then heard voices from out in the yard. Through the open front door she could see them walking over the grass. In front was Uncle Edmund, old and tall with a small head in a black cowboy hat. As he walked he wobbled on his ankles that he'd broken as a boy trying to rodeo. Behind him came a short old lady in a flowered dress carrying a little cardboard box.

"Hello Edmund," Grandma said, holding the screen door open. He looked down at her with his crafty scared look. He patted Grandma on the back and she patted him on the back and they stood there for a second with their arms crossed, making a stiff W. Then he reached out to hug Alberta and she breathed through her mouth to avoid his stuffy old tobacco juice smell.

"Lucille," Uncle Edmund said to Grandma with his crafty look. "This is my wife Adelaide."

"Howdedo, howdedo," Grandma said in the high cracky voice she got when meeting somebody. She was always in a flutter when somebody came and it wasn't until everybody had sat down and relaxed that she would say something mean.

"You folks should have come sooner for a bite of dinner," Grandma said.

Adelaide went straight to the kitchen to set out the canning she had brought as a present. She lined it up on the counter so the six quart jars of peas stood in a shining row. The peas in the jar were greener than life. It was a trick she'd learned from her mother but couldn't tell. At the bottom of each jar, against the glass and sitting up just perfect, was a little '59, carved out of carrot.

"Why those peas are too pretty to ever open and eat," Grandma said, her head trembling a little from politeness. Alberta could smell the particular kind of sweat that rose from her on social occasions.

"How do you get the carrot to sit up like that?" Alberta asked.

"Oh," Adelaide said. "That's a secret trick too."

"It's a winner," Uncle Edmund said, about the canning it seemed. "Yes sir, it's a winner."

He went out the front door like he was leaving but came right back in with a one-pound coffee can. He sat down in the old blue armchair where his and Grandma's father, Thomas Pratt, had died. Thomas Pratt had been too tough to lie down so died sitting up in that chair. Nobody usually sat there but Uncle Edmund dropped down into it, putting the coffee can beside his foot. Every so often, without appearing to think about it, he would lean forward, then, in a second movement, lean sideways over the can, spit tobacco juice, then sit back in the same two-part way.

Adelaide came back into the living room and went over to sit on the couch. She gave Alberta a round red-faced smile and said, "I see you up there," pointing with her eyes to the top of the piano.

There four pictures were lined up. At one end was Alberta as a naked baby. Next came Dad, when he'd been a pilot in the war. He was sitting in his plane, wearing a tight leather hat like a bathing cap, and looking at you in a jaunty way with one eyebrow cocked to show what a wild flier he was. Next was a young Grandma, standing out in front by the big tree. Her hair was in waves but she didn't look much different from now, stiff and tight already, her arms clasped across her chest as if holding in her heart.

At the other end of the piano was Grandma's father, Thomas Pratt, not in any real place but in front of some old-time photographer's painted clouds and white trellis. He was short with a beard and a mashed hat. But his little black eyes didn't have the scared look of most old pictures. He stared right back at you, as if knowing people would be seeing his picture for a long time to come. His right hand rested on the barrel of a long gun that stood beside him, like any minute he would pick it up and shoot back through the trellis.

"And there's your great-granddad," Adelaide said. "I've heard about him."

"Who's that? My dad?" Uncle Edmund asked, squinting up toward them with one old blue eye, so bright all of a sudden it seemed a shade over it had shot up. "I remember when that picture was took. I was right there."

"Where?" Alberta asked.

Uncle Edmund didn't answer but looked all around the room as if he'd switched in his mind to another subject.

Grandma came in now with two spots of rouge on her cheeks and said, "What can I get you folks," but they yelled, "Sit down, sit down," and said they'd just had dinner at the Swish Inn Restaurant in Adair, the town of population one hundred and ninety that was only five miles away.

"Say," Uncle Edmund said to Grandma. "Remember that fella Joe Meek?"

"No I can't say as I do," Grandma said. She sat down next to Adelaide on the couch but didn't lean back, her arms folded tight over her chest.

"He was one of those old sheepherders that used to hang around," Uncle Edmund said. "We just now went by the livery station up town and I was telling Adelaide how he disappeared there one night. I was up town the night it happened. I was right there on the spot."

"I remember hearing about it too," Adelaide put in. "Though I was only a child."

"Oh?" Grandma asked politely. "Are you from these parts?"

"I grew up in Burnt River," Adelaide said, naming a place on the other side of Bonner.

"Oh?" Grandma said, in a tricky voice. "You must have been a Lacey." Because the huge Lacey family, which Grandma hated, spread all over the county, with an especially big bunch of them in Burnt River.

"This old sheepherder come down from the hills," Uncle Edmund began to tell. "He was carrying his whole summer's pay. He went to the barber shop and had a shave and a bath. Then he went over to the livery stable where they ran a poker game. And after that, he was never seen again."

Uncle Edmund looked all around with his crafty sideways look.

"Oh well, I expect he left the country," Grandma said. "Like all those old no-goods finally did. This was no place for their kind."

"I know what became of him," Uncle Edmund said. "They took his pay and cut his throat."

Uncle Edmund looked around and Grandma said, "Fiddle-sticks. They didn't carry on like that when Papa was alive."

"The heck they didn't," Uncle Edmund said. "Those was rough times."

"They were not rough times," Grandma said, sitting stiffer. "They were the finest, finest times."

"Well, well," Adelaide said, winking at Alberta. "I guess they're over now anyway."

"Some folks always like to story," Grandma said, looking past Uncle Edmund and out the door at the bright summer yard.

"Then what did happen to the sheepherder?" Alberta asked.

"I'll tell you what happened to him," Uncle Edmund said, pointing his little old finger at her chest. "You dig right beside that livery stable. I'll bet you all the darn tea in China you'll find sheepherder bones."

"Pshaw," Grandma said. "Maybe they did like that at sheep camp when they got liquored up, but not down here in the valley where there were decent men like Papa."

"I guess not," Uncle Edmund said, pointing his finger at Grandma now. "I guess they didn't cut Hap Kizer's innards out at the Blue Goose dance hall and I guess my dad and I wasn't standing right there when he scooped them up off the dance floor all covered with the corn starch they'd put down to dance on."

This had more the ring of truth and Alberta could see Thomas Pratt in a dance hall, someplace long with a low ceiling like the Grange Hall. And there were the red innards in a pile on the floor, powdered white like stew meat dipped in flour. Beside it stood Thomas Pratt, with his steady black eyes and his long gun. With him there, everybody acted right, even with innards on the floor.

"Papa was never in a place like that," Grandma said.

"The heck he wasn't," Uncle Edmund said, fixing his good eye on her in a way that now seemed convincing.

"Well, well," Adelaide jumped in winking. "How's the church doing out here Lucille? You know my family's Methodist too." Adelaide winked sideways at Alberta as if to say, I'll butter up your old Grandma no matter what.

Grandma's father had built the church, so in a way it belonged to them too. But it had gone downhill. During the year there was hardly anybody in church, just a handful of old ladies, huddled together in the middle pews, Grandma sitting straight and grim in case the part-time preacher they had now said something wrong.

Grandma said the church was doing very well, though she wished they had enough to get a real Methodist minister of their own and didn't have to share one with the Presbyterians over the hill in Six Mile.

Adelaide said she was trying her hardest to get Edmund to go with her to church out in Bonner, now that he was getting older.

"You are living in Bonner then?" Grandma asked, trying to find out about their living arrangements with a sneaky politeness.

"Well," Adelaide said. "That's where I live. Edmund spends the week up at his claim, then comes down for the weekend. But I still can't get him to church."

Uncle Edmund leaned over to spit in the can, not appearing to listen.

"I don't know what ails him since he came from a religious family," Adelaide said, winking.

"That's a good question what does ail him," Grandma

said.

"My dad never went to church," Uncle Edmund said.

"Why," Grandma said. "Papa built the church. It's his church."

"He built it but he never set foot in it after that," Uncle Edmund said.

Alberta expected Grandma to tell Adelaide that Thomas Pratt had, though, sat up in this very blue chair and accepted Jesus before he died.

Grandma as a young girl had been kneeling by his side when it happened. Or maybe she had been standing in front of him, her hands clasped.

"He never set foot in the church and he never pussyfooted around the preacher," Uncle Edmund said. "Remember that hog-catching preacher, Lucille?"

Grandma didn't reply, her eyes looking upward, and Alberta said, "What hog-catching preacher?"

"Wellsir,".Uncle Edmund said, then moved forward to spit. "They had some new little preacher and he was drinking his tea in the parsonage one morning when one of the Laceys' hogs got away. The Laceys was hauling a load of hogs through town and the tailgate came open and one big old boar got out and went racing through town and everybody took in after it. So young Junior Lacey was in the lead chasing it past the church with a whole crowd behind him, everybody yelling, 'Catch him, catch him.' Well the new preacher heard the commotion and wanted to show what he could do. So he come running out from the parsonage..."

"Edmund hush," Grandma said.

"The preacher come running out of the parsonage," Uncle Edmund said. "'Catch him,' everybody was yelling, so the preacher jumped right on top of Junior Lacey."

"He was a fine young man," Grandma said, still looking upward, her head trembling slightly.

"I don't know about that," Uncle Edmund said with his crafty look. "But the preacher still shouldn't of jumped on him."

Grandma looked upward her head trembling slightly.

"Well, well," Adelaide started in again but Uncle Edmund butted in to say, "Lucille. Remember that preacher that got his head stuck between the posts of the church porch?"

"I remember some things," Grandma said, taking a deep breath. "I remember Papa and how things were. Papa was a Christian though he didn't have time to get to church. And we better just remember him."

"By god I do," Uncle Edmund said. "I'm the only one who does."

Adelaide finally jumped in to say, well, they were having trouble with their church in Bonner and when nobody replied went on, "They sent us a woman preacher."

"Oh?" Grandma said and it didn't register for a minute. Then she said, "No!"

Adelaide looked down and shook her head.

"Get away!" Grandma said.

Adelaide shook her head again.

"Why that is against scripture," Grandma said.

"A woman shall not head the church," Adelaide quoted.

"He built the church," Uncle Edmund said, "and he donated the land for the cemetery, but he never cared much for neither one of them. And he never cared for preachers, even the hog-catching kind."

"And," Adelaide said to Grandma, "do you know what she remarked when they quoted that to her, 'A woman shall not head the church'? She turned right around and said," and now Adelaide raised her voice to a high snippy one, "'Jesus is the head of the church.'"

"Law," Grandma said, in a way that was nearly friendly toward Adelaide.

"I'll tell you this by golly," Uncle Edmund said. "They had to carry him into that church feet first. He never went on his own steam."

"But he accepted Jesus before he died," Alberta remarked. It seemed somebody should set this straight.

"Who told you that?" Uncle Edmund asked, his one eye coming to life again.

Alberta looked at Grandma who said, "Certainly he did."

"Well, well," Adelaide said. "None of our memories are what they were," then told a story of how when her mother died, Adelaide and one of her sisters had sworn a man on a spotted horse had gone by on the road right before. But two other sisters who were out in the yard hadn't seen a thing.

Her mother had died, Adelaide said, from eating rhubarb and strawberries together when she had a delicate stomach.

"Well," Adelaide said. "Those times are gone now. Isn't that so?"

But nobody spoke up to agree.

"My dad never had a delicate stomach," Uncle Edmund said. He got up and wobbled out to the porch, taking his coffee can of spit with him.

Alberta got up and went out on the front porch where Uncle Edmund was sitting in Grandma's swing, holding the coffee can in his lap.

She sat down on the steps a ways from him and petted Mike. Pretty soon she said, "A cousin of mine is coming to visit from Japan."

Uncle Edmund though didn't seem to hear.

"Adelaide seems pretty nice," she said.

He still didn't hear and finally said, "My dad never went near that church on his own steam, I can tell you that."

"Oh you probably don't remember," Alberta said.

"Who? My dad?" Uncle Edmund squinted at her with his one bright eye. "I can see him plain as if he was standing right by that berry bush." The open eye shifted and he reached and pointed his little old hand toward the bush behind her head.

Finally she turned to look at the bush, which was full of tiny poisonous purple berries.

Uncle Edmund drew back his finger and spit in the can.

"Yes sir," he said when he settled back. "Nobody on earth remembers him as good as I do."

"How come the house burned down?" Alberta asked, hoping to catch him off guard.

Uncle Edmund looked all around the porch and then said, "I'll tell you about my dad. Did you ever hear of somebody leaving home when he was seventeen years old and being gone pert near twenty years and only writing two letters home all that time? That shows you what kind of man he was."

Uncle Edmund sat back, then leaned forward again to spit and said, "I'll ask you something else. Did you ever know anybody who could talk Indian? Well my dad could talk Indian. Talk to em, bargain with em, buy ponies off em. Taught me to talk Indian too."

"Say something then," she said, but he ignored it, fixing her with this good eye.

"He'd dicker with em. Once he bought a hundred ponies off the Indians for three dollars a head. Then he drove em to Omaha and sold em to the Dutchmen for two hundred a head. That's how he made his stake. Now I did a deal like that myself one time, but of course by then the Indians had raised their price and I didn't do as good."

Uncle Edmund spit and then said, "Say. I'm gonna show you something. Nobody knows about this but me."

Alberta got ready to jump, for fear he would pull something out of his smelly old pocket.

But he put down the coffee can and got to his feet, then went down the steps and headed toward the barn with his ankle-wobbling walk. In a minute she got up to follow.

"Now my dad," Uncle Edmund said, while they were walking through the barnyard dust. "He was a tough old cuss and he didn't have anything to do with all this church. He just wanted to be out making something for himself. And I'm just like him."

Uncle Edmund turned his head around to spit over his shoulder.

"Except you never got a big spread," Alberta said.

Uncle Edmund looked down at her sharply.

"And we don't have one either," she said, to show she wasn't bragging. "The Laceys are the ones that have a big spread now."

He walked on through the barnyard, not speaking.

"That's all right," he said finally, swinging up over the corral fence with surprising ease so she had to scramble to keep up. "My dad give the Laceys their first cow. They was in his debt like a lot of other people. They was under his heel."

"Who was under his heel? The Laceys?"

"Everybody."

Now they were at the sliding barn door and Uncle Edmund spit, then slid it in a practiced way, knowing just how to lift so it would get going. He probably still thought of this barn as his.

"My dad would loan a fella money to homestead," Uncle Edmund said, as the door slid open. "Set him up. But the fella lots of times wouldn't make it. If he did, fine and dandy. If he didn't, why my Dad got the homestead. That's how she's done. That's how I learned my business."

"What business? Gold mining?"

"Whatever business I was in, I learned it from my dad," Uncle Edmund said. "Take the blacksmith business. My dad bought the blacksmith shop one time and put a little fella in to run it. You can see the big old bellows up there in the loft to this day."

The old bellows were huge, wider than she was tall, ancient cracked leather covered with pigeon manure and too heavy to lift even one handle of. It had been laying in the loft forever like some giant prehistoric bug. She wouldn't be surprised if that was all he had to show her.

"Now my dad had a big place up to Sparta," Uncle Edmund said. "And one time me and him was riding in the hills up there looking for some cows that had got out. We saw this draw and my dad says, 'Let's just look up her.' So we rode on up, following a old creek bed. Pretty soon he stopped and got a little shovel he carried behind his saddle and dug around there a while, then he says, 'Why I think there's a big vein of gold here they missed.' Because of course they mined all over back in the 90s and it was all mined out. But now he says, 'Here's a vein, big as my arm,' so we took note of where we was and was gonna go back. Then before long he died."

Uncle Edmund spit back into the barnyard, then stepped up into the dark barn. He knew to head straight for the hole back by the manger where you could climb up to the loft. He climbed up and she climbed behind him and into the loft, stepping carefully when she got up there because part of it was floor and part of it was just hard pigeon manure and if you stepped on that you could fall right through to the milking parlor. Uncle Edmund knew how to walk up there too, testing each step, staying in line with the beams.

It was queer up in the loft, sickening in a way, with a crust of dusty pigeon manure on everything, and the pigeons cooing in a distant way, like to them you didn't exist.

"Now looky here," Uncle Edmund said, pointing his finger at a little circle on one of the posts that held up the roof. "See this wooden peg. My dad built this whole barn without using a single nail. Just these round wooden pegs."

"Why?" she asked.

"Because they didn't have any nails," Uncle Edmund said. "They had to do everything the hard way."

"There's the bellows," Alberta said, pointing to the other side of the barn. But Uncle Edmund went instead toward the other wall where some old trunks were sunk in hay and pigeon manure and he started trying to yank one open.

"They won't open," she said. "They're stuck shut."

But he got out a jack knife and started to fiddle with the lock and in a minute the trunk came open, its lid hanging with tattered paper that had once decorated the inside. It was all books and papers, some of them tied together with string and some just stacked up. Uncle Edmund got down on his haunches and started pulling some of the stuff out, old school books and what looked like checks and Alberta, leaning over the trunk too, began to feel sick from the dusty old rotten smell.

He kept on until he got to a package of letters at the bottom, tied with a piece of blue yarn. He unfolded the first letter and read it and when he was finished Alberta took it. But it wasn't a letter to anybody, only a poem written in a flowing lady's hand titled, "Our County." It went, "There is gold within her bosom, there is bunch grass on her hills. In winter, summer, autumn, her scenic beauty thrills."

"Some girl wrote that," Uncle Edmund said. "Lucille probably."

"It doesn't sound like her."

"Throw it out anyway. Now looky here," and he shook out for her an old letter, addressed to Thomas Pratt, Adair, Oregon, and dated 1896. It was written in dim pencil with bad spelling and there weren't any periods or capital letters. It started out, "tom for god's sake don't call that note rite now when the winner is so hard...."

Then it rambled on about notes and banks and was too hard to follow until it came to the end where it went, "tom i never saw such hard times as i have saw since i came i have actualy got to keep the children in the house this winner for want of shoes and everthing else in the same maner...."

"See that's the kind of business my dad done," Uncle Edmund said, taking back the letter. "Lucille doesn't know a thing about it. I was the one who knew."

He kept rummaging in the trunk, finally closing it up entirely and jimmying open another one.

She turned her back on him and the old trunks and followed a beam to the loft window and looked out over the barnyard and their two houses beyond, both shaded by the huge silver leaf maple tree Thomas Pratt had planted.

The whole farm would come to her. Maybe she would get back what they'd lost and own the whole valley. Then she'd get a big new pickup to drive around in.

When Martha Lee came, Alberta would bring her up here to the loft and scare her.

Or she would make Martha Lee go through an electric fence, warning her first that you would get shocked if you touched even the tip of the barbed wire fence. Only later would she show Martha Lee how you had to lie absolutely flat on the ground, face up, so you could see the lower wire and then wriggle under like a snake.

"Looky here," Uncle Edmund called to her. "This has been here since the day my dad died," and she went back to where he was pulling old black clothes out of the second trunk, two ladies' dresses, black and draped and one horrid black hat with yards of black gauze.

"This is all Lucille's stuff," Uncle Edmund said, "and my mother's." He spit, shooting a long stream to just miss the dresses that he'd put out on the hay. He pulled out a little man's suit that had a vest with a shiny back and a little pocket.

"This here is mine," Uncle Edmund said. "I wore this the day my dad was buried and I never wore it again. Nobody has touched it since. Looky." He pulled something out of the vest pocket, three gray kitchen matches and a tiny corner of a calendar that said 1912.

"Did you leave that calendar there on purpose?" she asked. "For somebody to find later?"

"See," Uncle Edmund said, holding up the vest. "I wasn't but a boy."

"Look if there's any money in the pockets," she said, but he didn't, instead digging some more in the trunk and finally coming up with something wrapped in white paper.

"Lucille doesn't know about this," Uncle Edmund said. "I'll show you if you won't tell."

"OK," she said. "Then let's go."

Uncle Edmund looked over his shoulder toward the hole in the floor as if he feared somebody might sneak up on him.

"They wouldn't come up here," Alberta said.

Uncle Edmund pulled off the white wrapping and held out something that looked at first like a long dog dropping. She shrank back, then saw it was a fat chain, as fat as two fingers, seemingly made out of fur.

"It's a hair chain," Uncle Edmund said. "A lady made it for my dad out of her own hair. Before he died he gave it to me."

Alberta took the chain and saw that it actually was hair, long and dark and coarse. Tied to it at one point was a red string and a carved red stone set in a gold locket. She opened the locket but there was no picture inside.

Uncle Edmund looked over his shoulder.

"Who was the lady?" she asked.

"I'll tell you who she was," Uncle Edmund said. "She was a friend of my dad's that not a living soul in the world knows about but me."

"Somebody around here?"

"Nosir," Uncle Edmund said. "Not a soul knows about it but me."

She handed back the chain and he wrapped it up in the paper again.

"The ladies always liked my dad," Uncle Edmund

said. "I took after him that way."

Alberta didn't say anything.

"Oh it's hard to say just why," Uncle Edmund said, as if she'd asked. He looked at the tissue paper package in his hand and finally put it in his shirt pocket.

"I'm the same age my dad was when he died," Uncle Edmund said. "So I guess I'll just keep this. Don't you tell."

Alberta felt inside the little vest pocket to see if there might be some money, but found instead a folded piece of newspaper and Uncle Edmund said, "Let me see that."

He took the soft old paper by the corners and shook it gently. He read the top, then gave her his craftiest look.

"Now here's something," he said. "Here's something you better not look at."

Alberta was ready to leave and didn't care whether she saw another old thing or not, but he handed her the clipping which was a newspaper story about some men chasing Indians who had crossed into the valley to steal horses. The men were chasing them back over Snake River into Idaho.

"Looky here," Uncle Edmund said, and he pointed to a place where it said, "Tom Pritt was at the head of the charge as they swam their horses across Snake River."

"Who's that, Tom Pritt?" Alberta asked.

"Why your great-granddad," Uncle Edmund said.

"Pritt? We're Pratt."

"Oh they just spelt it wrong."

Uncle Edmund was looking down at her, his one live eye gleaming.

"You better not read the rest."

He took the clipping back and folded it up. He put it back in the little vest pocket and put the vest back in the trunk.

They climbed down through the hole in the floor dangling their feet until they got a foot hold on the boards of the manger, then lowering themselves down. They went out through the barn and Uncle Edmund pulled the sliding door part-way closed behind them. It was a relief to be out of the dark barn and away from the old dead stuff. But Uncle Edmund stopped and looked all around the corral and she had to wait.

"I ran the place after my dad died," Uncle Edmund said. "I wasn't but eighteen when I took twenty carloads of cattle to Omaha."

She didn't reply, hoping he would stop talking and come on, but he said, "Oh that Omaha. I remember we stayed at the Crystal Hotel. Sidewalks twelve feet wide and such a crowd to crowd you right off onto the road. And here we was, in from a stock train, smelling to heaven. I remember we had to hike to the hotel, up a bluff and through the rocks."

He stopped for a minute, then said, "Thinking back, it seems like we must of went the wrong way."

Uncle Edmund looked all around the corral again, like he might see the right way to the Crystal Hotel.

"I'll tell you one thing though," he said. "I had plenty of money on me. And when you have plenty of money on you, it don't matter too much which way you go."

He was just an old bragger. But he kept standing there so Alberta finally said, "What about that gold you and great-grandpa found in Sparta. Did you ever go back and look for it?"

That woke him up and he slid the doors shut.

"Nosir. I been riding them hills for forty years looking for that draw again. But I never did find it. And it was gold in there too. My dad dug right into her and then he says, 'Why right here's a vein big as your arm.'"

"Maybe you imagined it," she said. "Once I thought I found gold in the ditch in a big rock. But when it dried out it was purple, not gold."

"Nosir," Uncle Edmund said. "I can see the draw now, plain as that big tree in the yard, and my dad said, 'Why there's a vein of gold right there.'"

"I wonder why you could never find it again," she said, as the jagged streak of gold shot like lightning through the sagebrush hillside. She raced toward it, Martha Lee close behind. They hit the rock one blow with a sledge hammer and the gold jumped loose. They bought tickets and new suitcases and flew around the world on an airplane.

"I always thought I would find it," Uncle Edmund said. "For thirty years I always thought I'd come across it if I rode these hills enough and every little bit I'd go back up there and hunt for it."

They walked through the barnyard. They could see Grandma and Adelaide who had come out front and were standing in the yard.

Alberta thought of telling him she would go look for the gold herself. Instead she said, "Maybe you could hire somebody to go hunt for it. Then you could split it fifty-fifty if they found it."

"Nosir," Uncle Edmund said. "That's mine and my dad's."

Before they got up to the front yard they could tell something had happened. Grandma was standing with her arms folded and her shoulders back. She was staring at the sky, her mouth tight. Meanwhile Adelaide apparently talked, her two hands waving. Uncle Edmund didn't stop but walked past them, his old ankles wobbling, straight to the car. He gave Alberta one crafty last look and patted his shirt pocket.

"Well, well," Adelaide was saying. "I know the Christian thing will be done."

Grandma, still looking at the sky, said, "I trust that it will Adelaide."

"I'm sure it will," Adelaide said, winking at Alberta.

"What Christian thing?" Alberta asked.

Adelaide only smiled and winked several times. Grandma stood still, her arms folded tight across her chest, while Adelaide said well, she guessed Edmund was ready to go. She kissed Alberta goodby and finally turned to hurry across the lawn.

"What Christian thing?" Alberta asked, when Adelaide was across the yard.

"Hush," Grandma said and she stood without moving until they had driven slowly off down the lane, a pillar of dust rising up behind them. Then she took her handkerchief from her sleeve and wiped the back of her neck and went back in the house. Alberta didn't follow, since it would be a while before whatever it was would heat up enough to boil out.

The hay trucks were way down at the bottom of the field now and there was nothing left growing by the house but a pale green stubble like whiskers that would scratch your ankles all up no matter how carefully you tried to walk though it. Still she should go down and tell Dad about the visitors from Japan. Then he would have something to think about as he rode around and around on the tractor the rest of the afternoon. It was a mystery what he did think about all that time. Surely not just the hay and the chopper and the trucks alongside. Maybe he went into long hot dreams as he sat on the tractor, the sun beating on his straw hat and the racket of the equipment cutting him off from any human sound. Maybe he put himself back to when he was a pilot in the war and flew so crazy he scared everybody.

But it was hot and the stubble would scratch her all up, so she went back around the side of the house to see if Mama was awake.

Mama though lay still as a log with the tin foil circles over her eyes.

So they had all given in to their own hot dreams and she could only climb to the low room over the cellar, a secret place, with a faint but sharpish smell. She propped a rocking chair against the door so nobody could sneak up on her, then lay down on the double bed covered with an army blanket to give in too.

In her dream she was somebody else than the one who would inherit the farm. Here she was somebody who would go away, an unknown person, dark and invisible.

The smells of Alabama, drifting from the boxes and books Mama had stored here, were the shadows of the other world and she breathed deeply of them, fearing one day they would fade and be lost. Smelling them she saw herself gone or at least not here. Once she had gone, to wherever it was, her mind would go blank so as not to picture Grandma chasing back and forth, on foot and in her old car, seeking the lost Alberta everywhere, her mouth in a thin, determined line, bending over to look in old pig sheds and under loose hay by the hay stacks, pounding on bridges with a shovel to make her come out. But Alberta would be somewhere else, not blinking an eye when she heard the whole farm, the houses, the barn, even the big silver-leaf tree had fallen to dust or gone to the Laceys.

She got up and went over to the closet where a cardboard box was hidden behind a wall of old clothes. She opened the box and took out the photograph album on top, then turned to the picture of a row of girls in long white dresses. They were somewhere in the dark, all holding candles, and the candles lit up their smiling teeth. The girl who was Mama in the picture, but now Alberta too, had the most glistening smile and the most beautiful dark wavy hair. Just outside the picture was another whole crowd of dark shiny people, women and men in suits, waiting for things to happen, things that couldn't be in the picture because until they happened nobody knew what they were. Alberta as Mama smiled her glistening smile.

Finally she put away the album and hid the box behind the clothes. She lay back down, seeing that Martha Lee might be the start of these things that were waiting to happen.

She lay on the bed in the hot close room, almost dozing, jerking awake from a dream that had a foreign tone but was too vague to remember. Waking she remembered a made-up boyfriend she used to have up here named Buford. He'd worn a red shirt with a row of pearl buttons down the front and he used to lounge in the doorway, smoking, and they talked and she loved the way he rolled his yellow cigarettes, pulling the tobacco bag string with his teeth. But she didn't want him now and she left him in the nowhere of those you've made up but won't imagine any more.

She lay on the bed a while longer, but it was about time to go if you didn't want to get paralyzed. Since it was the end she got up and went over to a cardboard box of old books. Deep in the box, carefully buried, was a thick hard-covered book with no paper cover called *King's Rose,* and on a page that the book opened to almost by itself there was a part that said, "He untied the strings of her bodice and opened it upon the pointed pink breasts, pink flowers yet hard as bullets."

She took a deep breath and put the book back and buried it again.

She went down and lay on the grass under the big tree, breathing the air that smelled of the silvery leaves. She turned to watch the tiny ants. They at least were not in some paralyzed dream, but rushing along the tree roots that rose up from the grass like little mountain ranges.

She too wanted to get up and go some place, to see somebody, to talk and brag and make things up and see if people believed it. If some stranger drove up she would tell him a big story. If the bald little Watkins Man drove up in his car full of spices and vanilla, she would run out and tell him her whole family had died and she was left all alone on the farm. Then she would start pretending to eat grass and see what the Watkins Man did.

If it wasn't so hot she would ride her bike down to

the reservoir and see if any Bonner people had come out to fish. They were strangers and you could probably tell them anything.

"I own this whole valley," she would say. "Get out or I'll sic my hired men on you." Then she would turn and ride off and leave them guessing.

Or she would drive down in the old jeep; that would make them wonder. She already drove all over the farm in it anyway, standing on the pedals when she needed the clutch or the brake.

But you had to push-start the jeep and there was nobody to give her a push.

The only person nearby to talk to was Ione Rexley down the road, so Alberta got up to go over there, first using the toilet, since Rexleys only had an outhouse. People said Ione was waiting for Old Man Rexley to die before she put in a bathroom. She was afraid to make improvements beforehand for fear the relatives would fight her for the inheritance.

Still Alberta felt kind of sorry for Ione who had gone away to California and then had to come back.

People said Old Man Rexley couldn't live long since he drove to the liquor store in Bonner every day but Sunday to buy a bottle of whiskey. At exactly three every afternoon you saw him driving by, slouched sideways against the pickup door, his old mouse-colored hat pulled down over his eyes, a little cigarette drooping from his mouth. Then at exactly five you saw him driving back home and they said he sat up and drank the whiskey all night and morning, finishing it just in time to get to Bonner again before the liquor store closed.

"Why doesn't he get a week's worth at once?" Alberta had asked.

"Oh I suppose he can't think straight anymore," Grandma said.

Ione Rexley was always home and glad to see you. The only time to stay away was milking time when she went into a rage. You saw her in the barnyard in high rubber boots, a man's jacket on over her dress, screaming at the cows and the dogs and her younger brother Johnny who wasn't all there. Seeing her then, the only hint you had that she had gone to California was her hair-do, a high pile she had fixed in Bonner once a month and then kept hair-sprayed in place.

So now Alberta went over there and Ione said from inside the screen door, "I wondered what went with you."

Ione usually had bushels and bushels of cucumbers to give away. Alberta took them to make whole towns of fat green people. On this day though Ione had just dumped all the cucumbers in with the hogs.

"I have a catalog for you though," Ione yelled from inside the screen door. "Come on in."

They usually sat at the kitchen table but Ione said, "Come in the front room for a minute."

They went into Ione's long, dark front room, where the light was cut off by overlapping sets of filmy curtains and by the glass shelves of African violets that sat in each window soaking up any sun that got through the curtains. It was a big room, but not big enough to hold all Ione's things, all the chairs and tables, couches and hassocks Ione had collected. Then, every flat surface except the chair seats was covered with a lace doily or a table scarf or an afghan, knitted in fancy patterns, such as a rose which had a different color for every row of petals.

Against one wall was a big table, covered with the little adult dolls, all in fancy long dresses sewn by Ione. You could see how some of their dresses had come from the same material as one of the pillows, or even two or three pillows for some of the multi-colored dresses. At the back of the room, the only bright thing there in the shadows, was a big square fish tank, lit with little light bulbs that shone through jars of colored marbles.

Beside the fish tank was Old Man Rexley, sitting in a brown arm chair the same color as his clothes. His was the only chair that didn't have doilies and he sat there like dead, his mouse-colored hat pulled down over his eyes and his whiskey bottle cradled in the crook of his arm. Even his little cigarette seemed to be out. He never looked up or spoke and Alberta didn't know if he knew somebody had come. Ione's Kirby vacuum cleaner stood upright beside his chair.

Ione led the way back to the fish tank. It didn't have ordinary gold fish but tropical fish, green ones and blue ones and pink ones that Ione had to go clear to Boise to get. Ione had learned about tropical fish from her former husband who she had lived with in California for three years.

They looked in the fish bowl where four bright-colored fish swam around and Ione said, "You know that blue fish the size of a silver dollar I got the last trip? Well, he disappeared."

"Where could he have gone?"

"You tell me."

"Did one of the other ones eat him maybe?"

"No," Ione said. "They can't eat anything bigger than a speck." To show what they ate she sprinkled in some fish food out of the box. The fish, bright as jewels, drifted upward to nibble.

"Do they jump?" Alberta asked, glancing around the shadowy tables and chairs. If he had jumped out you would never see him.

"No," Ione said. "He couldn't have gone anywhere on his own."

"Maybe Johnny got him," Alberta said. Johnny had gotten too old for school and just wandered around in a red earflap hunting cap, his rifle under his arm. But people always said, "Oh, he seems harmless."

"No," Ione said. "I taught him that the water would give him a shock."

"Anyway, if he had, it looks like your dad would have seen him," Alberta said.

"Oh Dad doesn't see anything," Ione said.

"He can't see?" Alberta asked.

"He can see," Ione said. "Like a dog or cow sees. But he can't make anything out of it."

"Can't he hear?"

"No," Ione said. "He hasn't said a word for a year."

She went over to him and yelled in his ear, "Dad! Dad!" but he didn't stir.

"His brain is just a wet sponge," Ione said.

"It's a wonder he can drive to Bonner every day," Alberta said. "It looks like he would wreck his truck."

"Yes," Ione said. "It looks like he would."

They walked back to the light part of the living room.

"Might as well sit down and have a cookie," Ione said. She brought out some cookies on a plate, macaroons, which had been her former husband's favorite. Alberta made herself a place on the couch amid the pillows. She kept an eye on Old Man Rexley to see if he ever moved or gave a sign he could hear them talk.

"We're having some company," Alberta said when they were settled. "They're in the Army. They travel everywhere."

"Of course my former husband was in every state in the union," Ione said. She was already at work on some embroidery on pale green cloth.

At least two thirds of the conversation at Rexleys' had to be about Ione's former husband, Eugene. He had traveled around in a blue Studebaker with a pole across the back from which hung all his suits and shirts. He had so many suits hung in back he couldn't see out the rear-view mirror and had to have one of those extra-wide mirrors attached to the car door.

"I know," Alberta said. "But our company's coming from overseas. Japan."

"Get out," Ione yelled at Johnny who had just opened the screen door and was coming in with his gun, his earflaps down in spite of the heat.

"He'll murder us in our beds," Ione said as he turned around and left.

"Oh," Alberta said politely. "He seems harmless."

"I woke up one night and he was standing over me."

"With his gun?"

"No, with my angel food cake pan."

"Why?"

"There's no telling what goes through his mind."

"Do you really think he might do something?"

"Oh," Ione said with a sigh, reaching up to fix a pin in the back of her fancy hairdo. "No."

"Martha Lee speaks Japanese," Alberta said. "And plays the violin."

"My former husband played the accordion," Ione said. "When he felt sad."

"Did he ever come here?" Alberta asked, forgetting, for certainly she had heard everything there was about Ione's former husband.

"Once."

"How did he like it?"

"He took one look and left the next day."

Ione had met her former husband during the war and for three years she lived in an apartment in California with the tropical fish he gave her. Usually he was away on trips but every day she did her hair up into the high black hair-do since she never knew when he would appear at the door. For her third anniversary she went with him on a trip from California to Texas and back. Then he left on another trip and she never heard from him again.

"Did he like your dad?"

"Oh he didn't let Dad bother him."

Alberta glanced at Old Man Rexley but he didn't stir.

"Dad can't live long," Ione said. "There's a dozen things he could die of. Stroke. Seizure. His liver go. Blood clots. The doctor said, 'I wouldn't be surprised if everything just gave out at once.'"

"Is he thinking about things, do you think?" Alberta asked. "Maybe it's like he's asleep and having dreams."

"Oh his mind's just a sponge," Ione said, looking down the room. "It looks like he'd want to die. It looks like he would want to take Johnny's gun and shoot himself."

They didn't speak for a minute, then Ione said, "Eugene drank one thing. Club soda. It's just fizzy water with no sugar or flavoring. I never developed the taste. But Eugene swore by it. He wouldn't drink coke since it ate out the stomach lining. He said the biggest hazard for a traveling man was his health."

At the other end of the room Old Man Rexley seemed to stir. Alberta looked at the clock over the doll table and saw it was five till three.

He shifted in his chair and finally pulled up to his feet and slowly walked past them, his whiskey bottle cradled under his arm so only the neck stuck out. He looked straight ahead as if they didn't exist and went out the screen door.

"Why doesn't he get a week's worth at once when he goes to the liquor store?" Alberta asked.

"I wish I knew," Ione said. "Once I went to Bonner and got five bottles myself. I said why fight it and maybe I could save on gasoline. I lined them up right beside his chair. But he wouldn't touch them. Still went every day for a new bottle. Finally I had to take every one back for a refund."

"Are you going to put in a bathroom after he dies?"

"Yes," Ione said. "Then I could afford it. Not having to spend half my milk check on liquor."

Alberta politely accepted this lie. She asked, "What color will you have it?"

"Mint green." Ione held up the green cotton she was embroidering. "These are the curtains."

"I wonder how Martha Lee will like it here," Alberta repeated. If you tried hard you could get Ione to talk briefly about your subjects.

"Your Martha Lee," Ione said, biting an embroidery thread, "will be so darn glad to get back in the car and drive out of here it won't even be comical."

"Oh I don't know," Alberta said. "I'll take her all around. I'll get the jeep going and drive her around in it."

"My former husband logged fifteen thousand miles a year in that blue Studebaker," Ione said. "Do you know how many times across the country that is?"

"Five times," Alberta said. She could kick herself for mentioning driving.

Just then they heard the roar of Old Man Rexley's pickup starting out in the barnyard and it reminded Ione to turn on the vacuum cleaner to vacuum off his chair with the hose attachment. Alberta took the chance to get up and go home.

At home everything was still silent and dead with afternoon, just the kind of place you would not want to visit for long.

She got a drink from the hose and then walked through the barnyard, climbed the three corral fences and got over to the mule barn, a little two-story barn that was another place just filled with old junk, old horse collars and saddles and horse shoes hanging on nails. Behind the mule barn was the little old jeep, topless and rusty, spattered with pigeon dropping, its seat a pile of rags to keep you from sitting on the springs. The key was in it, but when she turned it over, standing up on the clutch and gas pedal at the same time, it made only the lowest and sickest kind of moan.

If you could just get a push, it would run OK, as long as you didn't turn it off or let it die. You couldn't ever let your foot off the pedal.

She sat back down in the seat, as if she were going. She held the wheel and turned her head to the passenger seat, eyebrows high, as if responding to Martha Lee's questions.

Aren't you scared you'll run into something?

No, you can go around most things.

I would be scared to drive.

What's to be scared of?

Can you go anywhere but your own farm?

Sure. We can drive to my fort sometime.

Let's do it now, Martha Lee said.

So they would drive through the corrals, Martha Lee getting out to open all the gates, then across the road to the Laceys' field, which was big and dry, the grass all grazed down to nothing and burnt by the sun.

Once in the field they could speed up, bumping and jolting along like people really driving.

They kept driving across the field, going fast, bouncing over the bumps and little ditches, Martha Lee holding on for dear life.

Where are we going?

To my fort.

But what if somebody had torn down the fort, like some boys did once?

She climbed out of the jeep and went on foot back through the corral, climbing the three fences, crossing the road, then crawling under the wire fence into Laceys' field.

She set out across the long, hot field, heading for a spot where two trees grew close together, half a mile away, clear on the Laceys' far fence.

It was a field she knew well since she walked across it to get to school whenever she missed the bus. And when the Laceys were out in it working cattle she would climb the big tree and watch them like they were a show.

Wherever the Laceys went they went in a bunch, with the old man, Royale riding in front, either on horseback or in his jeep. He was a big man, with a round belly held tight as a watermelon by his white cowboy shirt. He had a fat red face under his cowboy hat and little wire-rimmed glasses. When they went by jeep, he rode along like a king, his oldest son Leonard driving, while he studied everything that was his. Behind would usually come another couple of jeeps filled with Lacey sons and sons-in-law and grandsons and nephews.

When they went by horseback, old Royale rode in front, his big belly in the white cowboy shirt appearing to float him like a balloon, so he sat his horse like he wasn't connected to the trotting underneath.

"Nobody brings more of a crowd to do less work," Grandma would say when the Laceys were across the road. She would stand at the window watching them all morning. When the Laceys hayed, she said, it looked like a county fair, they brought in so many people and rigs. And when they worked cattle it made her furious, the men all in chaps and neckerchiefs, hollering and yipping and showing off on horseback.

"Look at them cowboy," Grandma would say. Talking about the Laceys her voice would take on its nasty, sugary tone.

"What's wrong with it?" Alberta had asked. When Dad worked cattle everything was efficient, with the cattle coming through a set of corrals and finally into the chute that held them tight while they got branded and doctored. It was more efficient but not as much fun as the Laceys who worked out in the field, with a portable chute. The Laceys' cattle were always getting out so five or six Laceys had to go riding after them and trying to lasso them back. And you almost felt like the Laceys let one get away now and then just so they could get the chance to go tearing after it.

"What's wrong with it is they never saw a cow until my Papa gave them one. Royale's father didn't even come West until the railroad was built and he could sit all the way in a seat with his hands folded. And now look at them cowboy."

"Well, I guess they learned how," Alberta said.

Grandma had turned on her in a fury. "The winter Royale Lacey was born, his parents didn't have two dimes to rub together and they were living in a chicken coop. Royale would have died if we hadn't taken him and kept him warm on our oven door until he took hold. If we hadn't, you wouldn't see two dozen Laceys everywhere you look."

But Alberta liked to see them, liked to sit in the big silver-leaf tree and watch them cowboy. And she liked to see them feeding cattle in the winter when she had to walk across their field to school.

It was miserably cold those winter mornings, too cold for snow, just a hard ugly cold with the mud frozen in ridges and the grass and weeds breaking like glass under your shoe.

Then, nearly running, the cold cutting through her, she would see the Laceys, a whole loud gang of them, even though it was so early and miserable. They circled the field in their pickup, a couple of Laceys in the cab, a half dozen more on the hay wagon behind, their fat faces even fatter from the ear muffs they wore under their cowboy hats.

They rode with their legs spread to keep their balance on the rocking wagon and she watched them stagger like babies learning to walk, grabbing up a bale of hay, popping the twine with one jerk, shaking the bales off onto the ground, so the hay spread behind in a wispy green trail. The cattle wandered up to start eating and so formed a line across the field where the hay wagon had been.

In spite of the cold, the Laceys clowned, kept warm, maybe, by their fat, and every so often the one driving the pickup gave it the gun, trying to make the ones on the wagon fall off. The ones on the wagon would get a good footing so they wouldn't fall, then yell and hoot at the terrible driving. Alberta would keep her eyes glued to them as she hurried across the field and when they waved and hollered she waved and hollered back.

Now though, in this part of the summer, there were no Laceys around. Their cattle were all up grazing in the hills and they were probably off haying one of their other places. The big pasture was flat and empty, except for the half dozen duck decoys the Laceys put out every year toward the end of summer to attract ducks for the hunting season later.

Look! Ducks! Martha Lee cried, pointing at one of the decoys. Alberta had taken her by them on purpose.

Do you want to catch one? Alberta asked.

Catch a duck? How?

Easy.

Alberta stopped the jeep right beside the ducks and told Martha Lee to keep her foot on the gas. She jumped out and grabbed one of the wooden decoys. She tossed it from hand to hand. She got two duck decoys and juggled them.

Then she got back in and they drove on to her fort, which, when Alberta walked up to it was just like she left it. It was more of a tent really, made out of the hairy yellow twine that came from the hay bales and that Alberta had gathered from all over the field. To make the fort she had used the trees and the fence for three sides and made a curtain on the fourth side out of the twine. Inside there was a big stack of twine for a couch and a table of board and rock.

She went in and sat down on the couch and looked out at Laceys' field through the string curtain.

My great-grandfather taught me to make this. He learned it from the Indians.

The Indians had this kind of string?

Well. They used grass. Or rope. I can talk Indian.

I can talk Japanese.

So Alberta didn't say anything about other languages.

She sat on the couch looking out at the field and woke up to see something coming from the direction of home, a black dot that could be a dog or a person, possibly even Martha Lee, here sooner than expected.

But the figure, after getting some closer, so you could

see it was a person not a dog, didn't keep coming directly, but went slowly sideways through the field like somebody looking for something. It would go one way, then it would change and go the other way, and as it got closer it dropped to the ground for a few seconds. Then it would get up and come again.

Some kid, maybe, but it came closer and she saw that it was Johnny Rexley in his red ear-flap hat. Then she saw he was creeping along with his shotgun held down low in his hands and she went hot. He had tracked her here from the road and waited for her to get in the fort where she couldn't escape from the back and now he would kill her because he wasn't all there.

She jumped up, thinking maybe she could climb the tree and hide, but Johnny didn't seem to be looking toward the fort. Rather he was creeping in a kind of circle, keeping his head turned toward something on the ground.

Then she saw he was just trying to hunt the duck decoys. So she sat back down on her cushion to watch, seeing if he would ever take a shot or if he would keep waiting for a duck to fly.

Then it was nice sitting there hidden in her fort with something to watch.

She sat for a long time watching Johnny sneaking around and around the decoys until finally it seemed that he would stay there until dark waiting for the ducks to fly. He probably wouldn't shoot her, but it wouldn't be a good idea to surprise him either. Finally she slipped cautiously out of the fort and instead of walking straight across the field circled around by the fence. As she walked she kept her eye on Johnny who crept and crouched until she couldn't see him anymore. It could be he went out and hunted those ducks every afternoon and had been waiting for years for one to fly.

When she got back home it was nearly evening, and

the racket of the hay chopper had stopped, nothing rising from the fields now but the sweet smell of new cut hay growing damp as the day cooled.

The big tree drooped over the two houses and you heard the water going by in the ditch, a peaceful sound you didn't notice in the dead heat of afternoon when it seemed nothing moved or ever would.

Their grass looked neat and green, not burnt and scraggly like lots of yards where people didn't bother to irrigate. The only thing wrong with the yard, it was a little shorter on Grandma's side than on theirs since Grandma always cut her grass about four days after Mama cut theirs, making a clear line where their yard stopped and her yard began. Once Mama had sent Alberta over to suggest they both cut their grass the same day, any day Grandma liked, so the lawn could look unified. But Grandma seemed to like her grass looking different from Mama's and wouldn't go along with it.

As Alberta went between the houses, Grandma called out the back door and asked if she wanted to go catch potato bugs since there had been a lot of them earlier. Alberta said she would in a minute and went in to find Mama who she saw had been crying. Alberta stopped off in the bathroom instead of going on to the kitchen where Mama stood ironing. She turned on the water, washing her hands slowly.

Was she crying because it was not her coming from Japan on her way back to Alabama.

She was probably thinking of her last day in Alabama, a day you could see in the wedding picture that hung on the bedroom wall. In it Mama was beautiful and glowing with pink cheeks the photographer had added. She was coming out of the church in a white dress that floated like a Christmas bell. Behind were five bridesmaids all in hats the color of Mama's cheeks. Beside her was Dad, young and sharp-faced in his Air Force uniform, one eyebrow cocked, his two feet floating above the church steps.

Alberta went out of the bathroom and said, "What's wrong?"

She saw Mama stepping off the plane, coming down the steps with the same smile of the wedding, except this time she was carrying a suitcase and wearing her black dress with the white lace inset. Behind her came a girl out of the catalog, in a red and gray pleated skirt and a red sweater, carrying a shiny violin.

Mama said, "Nothing."

Crying, in a way, was part of her secret life. She almost never told why. Now she only said, "I was thinking about a reception for them."

"What do you mean reception?"

Surely people from overseas would not get a reception. Like Eleanor Lacey's wedding reception? With two bowls of punch, one spiked? Folding chairs lined up along the Grange Hall walls and all the little boys scuffling in the middle?

"Oh just a little party," Mama said, and took the finished ironing to hang in the bedroom.

But how would they find anybody to invite for Aunt Rae? They could invite Ethel, maybe, who was smart and read books and talked about all kinds of things. She probably even knew something about Japan. But she was gruff and rude and would fix Aunt Rae with a stare and snap, "Howdo!" when they met, in the exact same way you would say, "Shut up!"

They could invite Lu, who was fat and merry and always laughing. She and Mama would sink into giggle fits and nearly choke. But when it came to an actual conversation she only talked about gardening and canning. If anybody brought up anything else she would settle back smiling and when it was her turn to speak she would say, "My land!" in a sweet way, but you knew you were talking into blankness.

Or Ramona, who was smart like Ethel and could take an interest in things, but who worked out in the fields like a man in a sleeveless plaid shirt with big muscles.

She looked alright in her regular clothes but awful when she put on a dress and high heels and once at a church potluck beat all the men at arm wrestling.

There was nobody around like Mama, soft and pretty, so bright and laughing when company came.

The husbands didn't matter quite so much. Ramona's husband would do alright, he was tall and thin with a raspy voice and something held back when he talked that could let you hope he knew more than he said. Ethel's husband almost never spoke, in fact Alberta doubted if he would even come. She had only seen him at home by the wood stove in his socks. Lu's husband was the best. He was fat and merry like her, but he went on to make good jokes. After somebody had said something funny he would open both eyes and his mouth wide. Then he would lift his bottom a little off his chair and balance on his two bent legs, making everybody laugh more.

But would Martha Lee laugh? Or would she stare at them like they were freaks?

"I was thinking a barbecue in the side yard," Mama said, coming back in to put the ironing board away.

There was lots more room in the back yard and it was prettier there in the evening with the sun going down behind Sheep Mountain and the garden and the cornfield both green. But Mama didn't like to sit out there because Grandma could spy on everything from her kitchen window or stand behind her screen door listening.

"T-bone steaks," Mama said, "corn on the cob, sliced tomatoes. Maybe we'll borrow Lu's ice cream maker and have home-made ice cream."

"I could have a party for Martha Lee too," Alberta said.

"At home," Mama said, "there would be three or four parties a day for a visit like this. Somebody would have lunch, somebody else would have a tea, then a dessert, then a dinner and another dessert. Then others would invite them but they couldn't go formally, they would have to just run by and have a glass of iced tea."

Alberta was barely able to picture three or four parties a day, then running by several others and being polite and smiling at all of them.

"When I was married," Mama said, "I went to half a dozen parties every day for ten days. I had to wear something different to each one."

Alberta was silent, near disbelief. This could be one of the things Mama had started making up.

In the silence they heard Grandma's sharp steps, clip-clipping along the cement walkway that ran from her back door to theirs.

She got past and they heard the outside cellar door bang. In a bit she clipped back and knocked on the screen door, then put her hands up around her face to look through.

"Alberta," she said. "Are you in there?"

"Yes."

"Come pick these potato bugs. There's lots."

"OK," Alberta said. Grandma waited a minute but they were quiet so she left, then Mama said, "Did you tell her they were coming?"

"Yes."

"What did she say?"

"Nothing," Alberta said, because she never told either one what the other had said if she could help it.

She was going to pick potato bugs in a minute and earn some money but first she went back down to the barn and though she didn't like to be there much past bright day, she slid the big doors open and hurried back to the place where you could crawl up to the loft.

She climbed up, hurried to the second trunk and opened it and pulled out Uncle Edmund's little funeral suit. In the vest pocket she found the soft newspaper clipping about the thieving Indians. She carried it over to the light of the big loft window and gently shook it open.

The newspaper story started out in a windy old-fashioned way, telling how the men all gathered at somebody's ranch and swore that the Indians would have to be caught and how nobody knew what would happen next if this horse stealing was allowed to go on. Finally they got across Snake River and caught up to the Indians, Tom Pritt, her great-grandfather, in the lead.

She carefully shook and smoothed the old clipping and held it up to see how it would look hanging on the wall, maybe framed.

She read on to where they caught up with the Indians. Some of the men, although not Tom Pritt, were wounded and bled and it seemed the Indians had the upper hand. Some had to run and one fat guy said, "I can't go so fast. Don't run off and leave me," but the other men said, "Do your best. We're going to run as fast as we can."

Finally they got the horses. They killed some of the Indian thieves and ran the rest off.

At the end of the story it said, "They found one squaw and two papooses in the teepees. Tom Pritt wanted to dispose of all of them but the other fellows wanted to spare them. 'Ride ahead of me,' was all Pritt said, so they rode on and when he caught up with them he said, 'I have saved them from growing up to be horse thieves.' They saw there was blood on his trousers and didn't discuss the matter further."

Alberta folded the clipping back up and put it in its envelope.

She looked all around the barn and finally buried the clipping under the crust of old hard hay and pigeon manure against the far wall.

Then she hurried down out of the loft and went to kill potato bugs.

She went to the cellar and found a jar with a good lid, then walked to Grandma's side of the garden and started picking off the little hard red bugs, which she used to think pretty but had come to hate because of how they smelled when they were dead.

She picked for quite a long time because she needed the money and got her only income from jobs for Grandma. She had twenty dollars saved but wanted to have as much as possible when Martha Lee came. By the time it was getting too shady for potato bugs, she had the bottom of the jar covered. They stuck together, turning into a red squirming jam, already giving off a deadish smell.

If this were all, the potato bug job would be a good one because there was at least forty cents worth in here. But now she had to call Grandma and they would go out to the big flat rock behind the cellar. Grandma would shake out a few bugs at a time, enough so she could count, and then Alberta would have to smash them with a brick, smashing and grinding them on the rock until they were paste. This was what she had to do because Grandma said she had seen potato bugs appear dead but their shells were so hard that they weren't, and she had come back the next morning to see they had flown off. So they had to keep it up, letting out a few bugs, counting, then Alberta mashing and grinding them with the brick that was already red and covered with tiny wings and legs.

Only when the smell of dead bugs rose off the rock, and when it was certain none had escaped onto the ground or were trying to drag themselves down the side of the rock, could they go back in Grandma's and wash their hands several times and then Grandma would pay her. Alberta had asked once if they couldn't just flush them down the toilet but Grandma had said she wasn't certain where they would go in that case. Maybe it would somehow give them the chance to multiply.

On this day they smashed the bugs, only a disappointing hundred and fifty-seven, then Grandma gave Alberta an extra nickel probably because she was a little sorry she'd been that way about Martha Lee and Aunt Rae coming to visit.

Grandma asked her if she wanted a glass of iced tea with lemon and she said yes, feeling the power of the coming visit, something that didn't belong to Grandma in any way.

But when they sat down Grandma had forgotten all about the visit from Japan and said, "What do you think that woman had to say?"

"What woman?"

Grandma sat up straighter, her arms folded as if she were holding in her lungs, and Alberta could hear her breathing in and out.

"That woman of Edmund's."

It was getting a little dark now in the kitchen, though the sky out Grandma's west window was still pink. They sat at the table in the straight chairs and both watched the sky behind the mountains, behind a distant tree line. When Grandma was a little girl, she had thought the tree line was a row of Indians marching and now when Alberta looked at it, she could only see it that way, Indians always marching against the pink sky.

Against the pink sky now Alberta saw not just Indians, but the squaw and the papooses, marching along the ridge of the mountain, leading the pack horse behind them, happy to be going somewhere.

Alberta waited, unable to see Grandma's black eyes but hearing her hard breathing.

"She's already bought a tombstone," Grandma finally said. "A double stone with both their names and birth dates on it. So they can both be buried in the Pratt plot."

"Why does she want to do that?" Alberta asked. She got up to get the cardboardy ice cream cookies they ate in the afternoon, not very good but lightweight so as not to spoil their suppers. She didn't care very much at the moment who got buried in their plot. She cared more about parties, company and everything bright and pretty, with Mama making everyone laugh and smile. Not like Grandma. Whenever there was any social affair Grandma got jerky and too polite. She started to sweat, and said things that there was nothing to say back to, making everybody nervous.

So Alberta sat eating cookies, having this whole brightness Grandma didn't know about, and saw how she herself would know how to be easy and gracious at parties like Mama, not nervous and sweaty like Grandma. Sitting in the pink sunset she could see herself, as if through some crack, being lovely, not to haymen either, but to people someplace big and bright and crowded, possibly with people speaking French.

"Of course I don't begrudge him the companionship," Grandma said. "If that's what he wants."

"So what's the matter?" Alberta asked.

"I'll tell you," Grandma said, her voice shaking. "If he wants to marry some old party that is his business but...."

"She didn't seem like an old party," Alberta interrupted. In her mind an old party was more like Mrs. Robins who lived in a trailer up on the lot where the hotel had burned down.

"If he wants to marry her," Grandma repeated, "that is his business I suppose but when he wants to bury her in the Pratt plot next to Papa that is something else."

"Does he?"

"I don't know that he does, but that is her plan." Grandma made a deep snorting sound in her throat.

"Are any of his other wives buried there?" Alberta asked.

"I should say not."

"Did he try with them?"

Grandma showed he hadn't by giving another deep snort.

"Why does he now?" Alberta asked.

"It's her," Grandma said.

"'Edmund already bought the monument,'" Grandma said, imitating Adelaide. Her voice rose in a goo-gooey way, that was in fact a little bit how Adelaide talked.

"'It's got both our birth dates and there's nothing to fill in but the year we die,'" Grandma had Adelaide say. Then she gave one of Adelaide's winks and stretched her mouth into a big doggish grin. In the dark dining room, Alberta smiled secretly at how much it looked like Adelaide though it was mean.

She said, "Well, there's lots of room. Couldn't she be buried off to the side, not so close to great-grandpa?"

Theirs was the best corner of the cemetery, under the birch trees and in rich grass right by the irrigation ditch. They had such a good spot because the cemetery land once belonged to Thomas Pratt. Then, about the same time he built the Methodist Church, he donated the land for the cemetery.

Other people had plots with less shade. People who had come late to the valley had to be buried out in the middle where there was no shade at all. Finally they'd started burying people around the edges where the irrigation water didn't go and the sagebrush and cheat grass had crept back in. But in the Pratt part of the cemetery the grass was thick and the graves made a soft green mound that reminded you of somebody sleeping and covered with blankets.

There weren't many graves in their corner, just Thomas Pratt, his wife Net, and Grandma's husband who died before Alberta was born. That was all, and one time Alberta had stepped off how much space each grave took, stone and all, and had seen that even if they all died—Grandma, Uncle Edmund, Dad and her—there would still be half a dozen spaces left. Uncle Edmund's daughter Joanne would get a spot, though she had moved to Boise and worked in a hotel. Mama maybe, though you could not quite imagine her buried down there.

In any case, there was lots of room. There were hardly any Pratts. They weren't like the Laceys who had filled up their own corner, then branched out all over the cemetery, putting people anywhere there was a spot, so it seemed like there was a Lacey in every other grave.

"It's not that I begrudge the woman a burial plot," Grandma said. "If she's a Christian woman. But why doesn't she have her own plot with her own people? Why doesn't she want to lie by her first husband? It would be different if she and Edmund had been married all their lives, but here they are, too old to marry anyway."

"So Mama would get in?" Alberta asked.

Grandma looked out the window and finally said, "Well yes, by that time."

"Would the person I marry get in?"

"Certainly Alberta."

"What if it was a Catholic?"

"I don't expect you'll marry a Catholic."

There were no Catholics in the valley but there were some in Bonner where there was a Catholic school and Alberta had heard that the Catholic school kids drank and cussed. But she knew from books that in some places the Catholics were royalty, like the little child kings of France.

"What if I did?" Alberta asked. "Would they get buried in our plot?"

They discussed Catholics frequently, though not this particular issue, and Grandma said she truly did not know whether they went to heaven and it was a shame for the good ones, because of course there had to be good ones. But just the way they had it set up, it couldn't be right. For instance, if you sinned, all you had to do was pay money to the priest and you were forgiven.

"What if I did?" Alberta asked. "Would he get buried in our plot?"

Grandma looked out the window where it was dark now with only a pale blue layer laying along the top of the mountain and you could barely see the Indians marching.

"When someone marries a Catholic," Grandma said, "they make their wife or husband convert to Catholicism themself, so if you married a Catholic then you would have to become one."

"Then I couldn't get buried in our plot?"

"No," Grandma said finally. "Then you would have to be buried in some Catholic place."

"Would I still inherit the place if I married a Catholic?" she asked.

Grandma looked out the window and finally said, "Yes."

They sat in silence for a little until Alberta could think to say, "My cousin from Japan is Catholic."

"Dickens," Grandma said, because of course Martha Lee would be a Baptist like Mama had been and Grandma accepted Baptists.

There were no Baptists in the valley, but there were United Christians who Grandma accepted but didn't like. She didn't like that they immersed for baptism, rather than sprinkled as the Methodists did. For their immersions, the United Christians had a deep little well with two sets of steps, one going in, one going out, right behind their pulpit. It was usually covered with a curtain but if they had somebody to baptize they pulled the curtain back and filled the well with water. Then, at the end of the service, the one being baptized walked down the steps into the water in a white robe and the preacher tipped her over backwards.

"Oh they love to get up and make a show," Grandma said after every baptism. She went to their services after the Methodist services.

The United Christian church was bigger than the Methodist and had a vacation Bible school Alberta went to, and Grandma sometimes worried that Alberta would be influenced.

"Do they ever talk to you about immersion?" Grandma asked her once.

"No."

"If they ever do, you must say you have been baptized in your own church by sprinkling."

"In the Bible Jesus got immersed."

"Is that what they tell you up there?" Grandma had spun around to ask.

"No," Alberta said. "But he did didn't he?"

"Yes and he drank wine in the Bible. I suppose you want to do that too."

Of course they didn't mean exactly what they said in the Bible. When they said wine, you knew it meant grape juice which was what they drank at Easter communion. And she wouldn't want to get immersed anyway. She had heard about a woman who was electrocuted when there was a short in the heater keeping the water warm.

Grandma had always been religious, not, like most people, waiting to get religious when she was old. She had been a religious girl too and told stories of the revivals that used to come every summer. They would put up a tent in somebody's pasture and hold meetings for a week.

The main part of the meeting, and the part that stuck with Grandma, was when the evangelist would tell all the sinful things he had done in his life before he found Jesus. He had been a drunkard and had committed every other sin. He had neglected his family, talked filthy and gone to bad places. Nice people couldn't even imagine what all he had done. He had laughed at Jesus and mocked when he saw religious people.

But deep down he was miserable, and secretly at night when all the bad people were gone, he would look at the mirror and see himself, ugly and miserable. He would see the very devil looking back out of his red eyes. Then he would have to go out and drink some more and do worse things than before to make himself forget that the devil had moved into his body like a tapeworm.

Then somehow he was saved. Then the evangelist would begin to cry and everybody in the audience would cry and sob and even Grandma cried. More than that, she had told Alberta once, she would sometimes start to feel a little sorry that she was only a girl who tried to be good. Sometimes she would wish she had been a sinner too so she could have been saved.

"You wished you had been a sinner?" Alberta had asked, shocked.

"No, no," Grandma had said. "I was just a foolish girl."

But it was as hard to imagine Grandma a foolish girl as it was to imagine her a sinner.

"Will Joanne get into the cemetery?" Alberta asked now, referring to Uncle Edmund's daughter who ran a cigar stand at the Royal Hotel in Boise. Before going to Boise Joanne had married a rodeo cowboy, but they had soon gotten a divorce so there was no chance of him getting in the cemetery.

Once Grandma and Alberta had driven to Boise to visit Joanne. They had stayed in her little apartment and had gone down to see her cigar stand, right out in the lobby of the Royal Hotel, where she stood joking with all the businessmen, wearing a pointy brassiere under her fuzzy green dress and sea shell earrings.

"I don't know," Grandma said. "I don't know if Joanne is living a Christian life."

When they visited Joanne at her job and had dinner at the hotel restaurant, they found out that to go to the ladies room they had to walk through the cocktail lounge.

"That's how it is in Idaho," Joanne had said. "They don't have separate bathrooms for the restaurant."

"Well you should come back to Oregon then instead of walking past all the liquor," Grandma said, and she and Alberta had gone down the street to Alexander's department store to use the ladies' room.

"Do you think she stops and has a drink sometimes?" Alberta asked now.

"Certainly not."

"Did you think Gilbert was unchristian?" Alberta asked, referring to Joanne's boyfriend who was French and had shiny black hair that was stiff and didn't budge if you bumped it. Gilbert had seemed just perfect when he came to visit, lounging in Grandma's blue chair. He had long legs in slacks the color of oatmeal, with tan socks to match. Then it turned out he was already married.

"Gilbert is an example of what can happen," Grandma said. "When these girls go kiting off."

It was dark now in the kitchen and Grandma stirred as if to turn on the lights.

"Did you know somebody named Tom Pritt?" Alberta asked quickly. "Not Pratt but Pritt. In the old days?"

"I don't recall," Grandma said. "Why?"

"Oh I saw his name in some old newspaper in the barn."

"Edmund showed you a newspaper?"

"No. I just found it."

Grandma didn't speak and Alberta couldn't see her eyes anymore.

Finally Grandma said, "Yes I believe there was a Tom Pritt but he was never anybody we knew."

They sat for a bit and then Alberta said, "Are you going to make them take that tombstone back?"

"I don't know what they're going to do with it," Grandma said. "I doubt if they can take it back with their names already on it."

"Are you worried that she's a Lacey?" Alberta asked.

"A distant relative maybe," Grandma said, calm now after her blow-up. "She wasn't loud enough to be very much of one."

Now it was completely dark and they sat for a while.

Finally Grandma got up and turned on the light. They both squinted and stretched like they had been asleep, then Grandma started to cook her supper and Alberta went in the living room to look for ideas in Grandma's *Ladies' Home Journal* on entertaining guests.

But there were only recipes and hairdos in the ladies' magazines and Alberta turned to the *Reader's Digests*, one year's worth of which were kept on the bottom shelf of the end table, tended by Alberta, who threw out the year-old one each time a new one came. She turned now to "Humor in Uniform," thinking it might give her some clue to Martha Lee. But there was nothing about Japan and she turned to a story about a woman in a concentration camp in Russia who had made a whole alphabet by chewing up the bread they gave her, then rolling the bread into a long string, as if it were clay, and then forming the letters of the alphabet. Once the woman had made enough letters, she wrote things out, right in her cell.

This was what Thomas Pratt did, she could say, when captured by Indians.

But Martha Lee could ask, What did he write? Who was around to read it?

That reminded her of the story in the May *Reader's Digest* about a man lost in the deep, deep snow and how he stayed alive fourteen days by curling himself into a little ball far under the snow with just an air hole to breath through. Once he was there, he had gotten out all of his things, his food, his water that he kept thawed by putting it inside his coat, even a little notebook and a pencil. She pulled out May to see the picture showing him from the side, curled up in his hole eating a candy bar and writing in his book how he was surviving.

In fact, Thomas Pratt had been lost once, but in the desert. She didn't know what he was doing in the desert, but she had heard he was lost and run out of water. Finally he found some late at night. He drank and drank, then in the morning saw that it was green and slimy, an awful mudhole.

She got up to look at his picture on top of the piano, and seeing him staring with his little black eyes could easily imagine him drinking mudhole slime and not even minding.

But that wasn't much compared to surviving fourteen days in a hole under the snow.

Why not tell the snow story and say Thomas Pratt had done it on his way to Oregon? He took off right through the snow since he was so desperate to get here and start this farm that would come to Alberta one day. Then just pray they didn't have *Reader's Digests* in Japan.

PART TWO

It was the day before they were coming and when Alberta woke up too early, things were funny. First, she could not see out her bedroom window as she had every morning of her life, looking across the back yard and the field to Sheep Mountain, that was already blue and hot when she woke. Now her room and the whole house had been fenced in behind a white wall of sheets Mama had hung out from an early morning wash. Had hung, emboldened by the visit, all along the clothesline, far into Grandma's territory. Next there was the noise, too much for so early, of the washer chug-chugging, slipping back and forth on the kitchen floor, as if trying to escape. And the hired men, here early to try to finish the haying, were out in the barnyard, slamming doors and hollering. With dread, Alberta heard in their voices the promise Dad had said he was going to make them, that if they finished haying tonight he would buy them all the beer they could drink.

The closest she'd come to seeing anybody drink was Old Man Rexley in his chair with the whiskey bottle under his arm. But now she could hear drinking in the hay men's voices, a new, chilling note of recklessness, as if any minute their laughs would veer off into something dangerous. She feared even Dad might fall to some man's ailment, might get drunk and come home somebody else, possibly staying that way until the company came. Then everything would be lost in shame and disgrace.

Once he'd told her how he kept from getting drunk in the Air Force, when you almost had to drink with the other cadets. He'd drink, then to keep from getting drunk, go in the bathroom every half hour and throw up. But it seemed like a risky method, and she lay in the unfamiliar light almost wishing that the visit were over or had never happened, and that they could go back to how they had been, waiting and waiting for something to happen, but getting along all right when it didn't.

She got up and dressed in the shorts and shirt she had taken off last night, barely knowing her own clothes in a room with the back yard gone. She went out in the kitchen which was loud and steamy from the wash, took her oatmeal from the pot on the stove but did not go to eat on the back step, as she usually did on summer mornings, since Mama was going back and forth through the door and you had to just stay out of her way and try not to talk. She had been too busy to say much in the whole week since the letter came, involved in the complicated effort of getting ready for such sociable company.

Alberta ate her cereal in the dining room but it was only a little better, now echoing and bare. The ruffley white curtains had all been taken down, and without them there seemed no protection from the barn which stood up big and rough across the barnyard.

Inside the dining room there was nothing to suggest their own life. There were no boots or shoes or socks behind the stove, no catalogs stacked by the rocking chair. The top of the buffet had been cleared and all the clutter of circulars and sewing things, pencils, scissors, pretty stamps, lists, things which didn't have any home of their own, everything was gone, replaced by one glass candy bowl, empty under its sharp lid. It was a bowl she had never seen out before but knew was one of the wedding presents.

Then, the mound of farm magazines, full of broadside Herefords and odd, Midwest farmers in caps rather than cowboy hats, had vanished from under the radio. Now the radio table was empty, showing a pale red bottom shelf that had never been seen before. In fact, everything they had ever looked at or held in their hands was gone, there was nothing to show it was them. They could be teachers. They could be a new preacher's family just moving into the parsonage.

Even the red tweed davenport had been scrubbed and scrubbed with special soap and had been too wet to sit on for days. It was in fact still wet, and now it seemed would be wet when the company came. The davenport was maybe, a little brighter, than it had been before but the big round spot a little right of center where Alberta had thrown up as a baby only seemed to stand out more, and after scrubbing and scrubbing Mama had cried over the spot. Grandma said Mama should have gotten the stain up when it was new, not ten years later, a remark Alberta did not repeat. Dad said she could cover it with a blanket, like lots of people covered their davenports, but Mama flared that she would not live with a blanket over the davenport or a plastic cover either. Because lots of people, when they got a new davenport, would put it into a plastic cover so that several years later it still looked brand new under the plastic. And almost everybody finally covered their davenport with a blanket. But Mama had told Alberta, never never do that. To do that is to give in completely.

She finished her oatmeal and then went up over the cellar, where she and Martha Lee would sleep, with Aunt Rae taking Alberta's room. She had to clean it up and put sheets on the bed. Also she had to prepare for the party she was going to have for Martha Lee and to which she would invite her Sunday School class.

She crossed through the bright soft morning, a morning on which they would usually all find themselves outside with some job or interest just to be in the air and to look at Sheep Mountain shining blue. But now there was no time for a soft morning, and she climbed the ladder up the side of the cellar. For the first time she noticed how the dark landing outside the cellar door was stacked high with junk. Junk, there was junk everywhere on this place. Was that all they had ever done here, just store up junk? Just save every old book and dress and stupid shoe? When it was hers she might just build a big fire and start over fresh.

But right now she could not plunge into any dark pits of dust and old things, even to stack and straighten and know what was there. She went into the room where she and Martha Lee would sleep. It was dark and gloomy in there, even on this bright morning, its one little window blocked by a dirty blue curtain that wouldn't slide back.

It smelled dark too, dusty and of old rotting things, and the strange sharp smells of Mama's Alabama box could not cut through. The crepe paper streamers she had hung for the party seemed to make it worse, the bright red and white only showing up the oldness and darkness.

Alberta cried, as Mama had cried at odd times all week, but she stopped because there was no time. They were coming tomorrow, in fact tonight, at three a.m., and sometime in the dark they would bring Martha Lee up to put her in bed with Alberta who would be awake, but would pretend not to be and could that way observe Martha Lee. It was only the idea of this secret watching that allowed her to swallow not getting to go to Bonner with Mama and Dad to meet the plane, since the car would be too crowded with all the luggage.

Also she had to go ahead with the party because of the crepe paper, costing forty cents a roll, eighty cents for two rolls, which could not be returned now that it was hung.

She had allowed only two hours for the party, from two to four next Tuesday afternoon. Her plan was that the Sunday School kids could be sent home at four and she and Martha Lee would join into Mama's party. But how was she even going to fill two hours?

What a relief to give the whole thing up, but there was that crisp crepe paper.

So, what would they do after they came up here and saw the crepe paper? There were no presents to open, no refreshments. She had turned down Grandma's offer of help, except for buying the crepe paper, because she wanted to be on Mama's side, not Grandma's, for parties.

Maybe she would have them sit around a flashlight campfire and tell stories, and she went down immediately to get newspapers and tape, Grandma's flashlight and one of her own red socks. She went out to the ditch to pry up several rocks. Back up over the cellar she taped the newspapers over the one little window, arranged the rocks in a circle on the floor and set the sock-covered flashlight in the middle to act as a campfire. She closed the door and turned on the flashlight and it looked quite a bit like fire.

So, they would sit around the campfire, with each person having to tell a story, and all the worry would then be moved from her to them. They would have to come up with the stories, Martha Lee too, with everybody watching and judging, seeing whether she was too shy to say anything or whether she told something stupid that wasn't any good. Then if she couldn't tell a story nobody would worry about her any more.

Alberta could tell good stories. She would start with general ones, such as the couple necking in the car who hear the sound and drive off fast and then get home and see the murderer's hook hand on the door. If that went OK, she could tell about Thomas Pratt. How he had curled up under the snow to survive with only a quarter cup of water and a chunk of jerky the size of your finger. How he had a little New Testament with him, a red-letter Testament, and had decided to memorize all the words of Jesus and each time he memorized all the words in red on a page, front and back, he would eat it.

But maybe it wouldn't make such a good story to have him religious. Maybe it would be better to have him tough and wild and when he got caught in a blizzard he would have to kill his horse. He would cut it open and crawl inside with all the hot horse innards and lie there until the blizzard stopped, then walk home all bloody.

How had that man buried in the snow been able to see? From the drawing in the *Readers Digest* it looked like he could, the way his things were spread all around him. Maybe the light came down through the snow. She would claim the light came down through the snow, but also she would have him with a pocketful of kitchen matches which he would light, one a day, then hold against the snow wall, melting it so he could lick and this was how he got extra water. Alberta curled up on the floor, held up a pretend match and licked.

Maybe she would tell a story of how their first house had caught fire and burned down, the house built by Thomas Pratt, the finest in the valley. Say someone accidentally tossed a match in where Thomas Pratt kept his bullets and caused them to shoot off and start a fire. They shot right through the house windows, and exploded like fireworks above the big tree.

Or it was Grandma as a little girl who started the fire and then ran out of the house to sit on the quilt and watch, and nobody guessed to this day it was her who did it.

Thomas Pratt started it himself so he could run off with the lady who gave him the hair chain.

Or it was Indians, burning down Tom Pratt's house because they were mixed up over who killed the squaw and papooses.

Well, she would say that some old sheepherder had come in, dropped a match by the gunpowder and caused it to go off. Then they had all run out of the house in their night gowns because it was about three in the morning. And each had time to take only one thing. Grandma took her Sunday shoes. Uncle Edmund took his boots and spurs. Thomas Pratt carried out the big blue chair that he would before long sit in to die in a rented house in town.

And if Martha Lee's stories were such amazing stories of Japan and the Army that everybody sat with their mouths open?

Then she would tell about Thomas Pratt killing his horse and maybe even eating the raw horse liver to stay alive.

If none of that worked, there would still be the breasts like bullets.

By the time Mama called her to help with dinner, the party seemed set. She went down and set the table and got the basin and was happy when she saw the hay men had come up from the field crammed into Hank's black Buick, showing that haying was going OK. If one of the rigs had broken down they would drive up more grimly in the pickup.

But now the coon tail was waving and they rolled up kidding Hank about his car, which had, besides the coon tail, a rabbit's foot hanging from the mirror and a shiny green suicide knob on the steering wheel so Hank could put his arm around his girlfriend and still drive.

Yesterday they had joked all during dinner about how Hank's car needed new brakes and how the brake job had caused a six months' delay in Hank's wedding to his girlfriend, Shirley Duncan. Then, when Shirley said, "It's that car or me," Hank had gone out and rebuilt the carburetor.

Every day there was something new about Hank's car, often involving his courtship of Shirley, and Alberta was trying to think of some jokes of her own to kid Hank with at dinner. He was tall and thin and always called Alberta, Bill. She didn't think he really wanted to marry Shirley, who was milky white and plump as a toad with long blonde hair she was always brushing or fooling with somehow. She was in high school and one of the new people who lived in the trailer court so nobody knew who they really were.

As the men drove up, Alberta was doing the potatoes, getting the big pot off the stove, pouring off the water and mashing them with the electric mixer, putting the beaters on slow and ramming them against the big lumps of potato until they broke enough to turn the beaters higher. She poured in milk, then turned the beaters up and whipped in a way Grandma said made them too slick like glue. Grandma had mashed hers all by hand, even when there were twice as many hay men and only a wood stove to cook on. Alberta could picture her, red and sweating, mashing a dishpan-sized pot of potatoes, furious as if it were full of snakes.

The potatoes mashed, she left them in the pot to stay hot and carried a bucket of cold water out to the wash basin and a tea kettle of hot water and filled the basin half with each.

The men were all black-faced from hay dust, and telling each other to wash good since they didn't want to dirty Hank's back seat up for him when he was going to need it tonight. Going back, they said, they'd all sit on their handkerchiefs.

"Need it for what?" Alberta asked DeWayne MacIntosh, who came to wash first. DeWayne was tall and thin like Hank, but he had whitish blue eyes and his face sloped straight back from his mouth to his Adam's apple with no chin. And it made her nervous the way he ate. He seemed not to chew, just to put it in and swallow, and with his eyes and no chin he seemed a little snakish.

"Need it for what?" she said again, since DeWayne didn't answer.

"He needs it to take Shirley to the movie," Dad said, and they all laughed in a certain way so she saw it was something they couldn't say in front of her.

Then Hank said, "Aw I rather take Bill to the movie but she won't go with me."

And DeWayne said, reaching for the towel, "Least

they teach them something in school these days." Alberta blushed, busying herself dumping out the basin, then filling the basin again from the tea kettle and bucket.

Next to wash was Junior Baird, the stacker and so the dirtiest, and the one Alberta tried to remember to be kindest too. He was short and had bulging muscles everywhere, his arms in a cut-off sleeved shirt were nothing but muscles sliding under the red skin. On anybody else the shirt would be an embarrassment, but everybody said, "Poor Junior," since he had a very bad stutter and also because he had wanted to join the army but failed the mental test, then felt so bad he wrecked his car. But he was a good stacker.

Junior snorted and blew in the wash water in a disgusting way, but Alberta tried to overlook it and to watch at the table to see whether he was looking at the bread or the potatoes so she could pass them before he asked because he always got stuck on the p of pass.

Hank, though, had brown eyes and a fine chin and she loved to see him dunk his longish brown hair in the basin and then give his head a flip so the hair would all fly back smooth. She loved his long hair but at dinner they would kid about hair clogging the hay chopper and they said hair in Hank's fuel line was probably all that was wrong with his car. They said they kind of hated to eat dinner around Hank with hair flying everywhere so one day he wore a hair net and everybody about died.

She watched Hank wash, noticing how he didn't snort and blow in the water but washed in a more delicate way, first getting the black off his hands, then washing his face and even getting his soapy hands behind his ears and around his neck. He took the towel and dried in the same delicate way, not scrubbing like Junior did but patting himself.

Instead of fat bulging muscles everywhere he had a smooth little mound of arm muscle, rising up out of his brown bony arms.

If he weren't so much older she could marry him and they could run the place together once Alberta inherited it. After a day's work they would go out and drive around in the black Buick, with the windows down and the smell of their own new hay blowing in on them.

He saw her watching and said, "What's up Bill?"

"Oh," she said. "I'm having a party for my cousin from Japan."

"Well I didn't receive no invitation," Hank said.

She tried to think of something smart to say but couldn't.

They sat down at the table, Dad at one end, Mama at the other. Mama, in spite of the confusion of the morning, was calm and smiling, and had even put on a new dress, turquoise with a square neck a little low that showed her brown skin. It was a made-over dress, from something in the big package of clothes the aunts sent every year from Alabama. This Alabama package was one way Mama always managed to look different from everybody here.

Now it was Mama who led the conversation, asking the hay men things, then spinning whatever they said out into something bigger and more interesting in a way that seemed almost magical. She made even Junior want to talk and he held them up for five minutes trying to tell about the new car he was going to buy. Alberta was embarrassed but Mama kept on and finally it came through that Junior had gone shopping for a new car and when the fella asked whether Junior had anything as a trade-in Junior told the fella his old car was a wreck. And so, Junior finally got out, the fella said, "Oh, you must be ha-a-a-a. . ." and Mama said, "Hank Hopper?"

Junior nodded, all red, and everybody laughed, and Alberta saw how Mama had gotten this big laugh for him, and also how she glowed at the head of the table. Whereas Alberta was too much like Grandma, nervous and tight, not soft and glowing.

"I hope you aren't going to have Grandma's tight mouth," Mama sometimes said. "I hope you aren't going to go at everything like killing snakes."

Grandma on the other hand would say, "I hope you aren't going to have a wide bottom like your mother's. I hope you aren't going to like lazing around."

Whereas Alberta herself feared she could turn out nervous and lazy both. With a tight mouth *and* a wide bottom.

Then it was dessert and she brought out the pieces of pie, taking the dirty plates back to the kitchen. DeWayne MacIntosh lit a cigar and gave Dad a cigar and Hank and Junior took out cigarettes. They all sat back and started talking some more about what Hank was going to do to court Shirley tonight, whether he would take her to Bonner to the Chinese restaurant or whether they would go down swimming at the reservoir after dark when it was more romantic and you couldn't see the green scum that grew on the water. Alberta pictured Shirley, pale and plump in a white bathing suit, dipped in the green water of the reservoir and coming up dyed like an Easter egg.

"Say I bet Roy was quite a courter," DeWayne MacIntosh said to Mama. Dad looked down at his cigar as if he was trying to remember and didn't know they were all waiting for him to tell some story of wartime as he almost always did after dinner unless one of the rigs was broken down.

"I do remember one time," Dad said finally, leaning back. "I was courting Margaret and I wanted to send her word that I'd be over that night. So, like I always did, I was going to fly by and buzz low over her house."

Dad looked up in the air as if looking for himself in a little plane, buzzing like a bee in the pink Alabama sky.

Alberta looked up to see herself as an airline stewardess in a blue suit, high heels and little wings on her chest.

"Well they had one old policeman in this little Alabama town," Dad said, "and he didn't like me coming in low all the time. He would always report me and try to get me court-martialled."

Dad looked up again and they were all quiet with only the cigarettes going in and out and the idea of the little plane buzzing high in the air.

"Well," Dad said finally, looking now at DeWayne and holding out his hand as if to keep DeWayne still. "On this day I happened to notice the old fella's blue car parked on main street and him out beside it, staring up at me and fixing to go report me again. So I went ahead and buzzed Margaret's house like always, then when I finished, I flew over to the edge of town where there was a row of trees. I dropped down behind those trees and flew for a while until I was in the next county. Of course this old fella thought I must of crashed. He went and called up the ambulance and the fire department and the whole town went tearing out to see the charred remains. I guess they hunted all afternoon."

"That must have been a disappointment," DeWayne said, and everybody finally laughed but softly.

The hay men sat without moving, only their smoke circling over the table.

"So they never caught you," DeWayne said finally.

"Oh yes," Dad said. "They got me. They court-martialled me for buzzing a parade ground when a general was there. Me and a whole wing but I was in the lead so I'm the one they court-martialled."

"Why did you do that?" Alberta asked, not able to remember, though she had surely heard the story lots of times.

"Well I didn't know there was a general there," Dad said.

"But why did you want to buzz it anyway?"

"Well we'd just graduated from air cadets and gotten our orders," Dad said. "And they'd made me an instructor. But I thought if I acted kind of irresponsible they wouldn't want me for an instructor and I could go to war."

"Sounds like it might have worked," DeWayne said.

"Well it didn't work," Dad said. "They were going to take my wings if I didn't fly right."

"So what'd you do?" Alberta asked.

"I flew right," Dad said, reaching for his hat. "And I never got to war. Where's that gallon water bottle. Let's go."

But it turned out they'd left the bottle at the stack and Dad told Alberta to ride down with them and get it.

"I don't want anybody dying of thirst," Dad said. "Not till we get the hay up anyway."

"Aw," DeWayne said. "You just want to fill us up on water so you won't have to buy so much beer later on."

Dad said to Alberta, "Come to think of it, bring two gallons of water, one now, one about quitting time." So they all went out with jokes about water versus beer and Alberta got to go with them, happy to leave Mama with all the dishes.

She got in front between Dad and Hank. DeWayne asked if Hank thought his car could handle the extra fifty pounds.

"I planned to stay in second gear," Hank said.

"That's a good idea," Dad said. "Don't take any wild chances."

Alberta said she would be glad when they could ride in Junior's car and go faster. Hank said, "Bill, I thought you was my friend,"and so they rode down the lane to the field.

Hank drove in the gate and parked in the shade behind the stack. The stack was round as a tin can with a little fence of wire and slats circling it that the stacker would get inside of, then stomp the chopped hay tight until it bulged out through the slats. When the hay was as high as the fence he would pull it up a foot or so and stomp in more hay and so on until, like now, the fence was up higher than your head and you could see the lines on the packed hay below where the slats had been. Now Junior got the elevator going, which was a long trough with little moving dividers that carried the hay from the truck up to the top of the stack. Junior climbed up on top and started to stomp the hay down harder, getting ready for the next load. There was only one narrow stretch of field to cut, about six loads worth.

Dad started the chopper that was parked in the field where they'd quit before dinner, then climbed up on the tractor. Hank got in the old green Dodge truck and started it and she got in to ride one round with him before she went back up with the water bottle.

Hank swung out so she could get in on his side since the other door didn't open. She climbed in past the shotgun he kept behind the seat for shooting pheasants and got clear over to the other side, pressed against the door so as not to sit in the hole where the seat's foam rubber insides had come out. It was hot inside the truck, sticky with little pieces of chopped hay. Hank pulled up so the bed of the truck was under the high spout of the chopper and they started to crawl along, the chopper making so much noise when it hit the hay and started to chew it up you couldn't hear to talk.

She sat with her arm out the window, watching for the old doe that had been living in the hay field all summer. Sometimes they would see the doe on the edge of the field, standing still as a tree, her head up, staring. Then as the chopper came close, she would bounce off to hide further back in the hay field. Pretty soon though they would have to cut the last rows and then she would have no place left to hide.

"Where will she go?" Alberta yelled at Hank over the racket.

"Back up in the hills I guess," Hank yelled, the blackish hay dust already sticking to his sweating face.

"Is that gun for deer too?" she yelled. She'd only seem him shoot chinee pheasants.

Hank shook his head, concentrating now on keeping the big old lumbering truck right beside the chopper as they turned the corner at the top of the field.

She pictured a chinee pheasant exploding up out of the hay in front of them, how Hank reached behind the seat for his gun, threw open the door and took aim, one foot on the running board of the truck. He tossed the pheasants to her and she carried them to the house, their heads wobbling under the slick brown feathers. She came into the yard with a pheasant in each hand and shook them in Martha Lee's face to scare her and to show how tough it was out here on a farm.

She rode beside Hank, dozing almost in the hot scratchy noise, until the truck was full and DeWayne was pulling up behind. Dad raised his hand to wave Hank ahead and DeWayne pulled in at just the right second so only a light green skiff of chopped hay fell on the ground between their two trucks. Then Hank shifted gears and they jounced across the field to where Junior was waiting on the stack, stomping idly, his red muscles popping in the sun.

When Hank got the truck backed around the stack, Junior came down and lifted the bottom end of the long elevator trough up, shoving it under the hay in the back of the truck and then turning the elevator on so the little piles of hay went riding along, between the slat dividers, to the top of the stack. Before the first pile got there Junior had scrambled up on the stack and was standing waiting with his pitch fork. Hank climbed up in the back of the truck and so did Alberta. He handed her the broken-handle pitch fork he carried for a spare that was just about her size, and took the good one for himself. They both pitched the hay toward the elevator, which had quickly carried off all the hay close to it.

Alberta pitched as hard and fast as she could, seeing how it would feel to have the place belong to her and to feel desperate to get the hay up before it lay in the field too long losing its juice.

If she married somebody like Hank, would the place be half his, or would he still be a sort of hired man? Nice as he was with his delicate manner and joking way, she couldn't imagine giving half of her great-grandfather's place to him.

They pitched until the truck was empty and used their feet to scrape the last bits into a pile for Hank to get one last fork full. Then they got down from the truck and Hank winked at her and drove off.

It was hot and the pitching had worn her out so she decided to cut through the cornfield instead of going around by the lane. She found the gallon water bottle where they had left it on the shady side of the stack, wrapped in a cheesecloth bag. She dumped out the last cup of warm water and then put the bag over her shoulder and started the hot walk to the house.

She walked back across the short end of the hay field, now stripped so you could see clear up to the barn. As she neared the cornfield, the hot sweet smell of the hay field gave way to the hard green smell of corn, a smell like new concrete, or something else hard, not like anything to eat. Yet when they chopped the corn into silage and put it in the silo it oozed sour juices and gave off steam. She and Dad would both chew on a piece when she rode with him to feed the cattle, her steering the tractor while he shoveled silage off the wagon.

"Don't get drunk," Dad would say, since the reason it steamed was that it was fermenting just like liquor. And whenever a steer in the feedlot would act crazy, swinging its head or bawling too much, Dad would yell, "Look out, look out, there's one that ate too much silage." And when she was littler, still half believing it, she would stiffen up behind the wheel of the tractor for fear the drunk steer would cause her to wreck.

Now, she stood at the edge of the cornfield and looked back across the hot hay to Junior on the stack, to the chopper and the trucks. She hated to leave them with all their fearless noise, but finally you got tired of the racket and dust and hay down your neck, no matter how much you liked it. And they needed the water bottle filled, so she pushed aside two corn stalks and stepped inside.

Inside the rows of corn it was a dark jungle, the stalks growing close together and twice as high as your head, blocking out the sky. The minute you stepped in, the big leaves would grab you, sticking with some special stickeryness they seemed to have for just this reason.

The leaves clattered when you moved, right in your ears, and you could try to either duck, so as to get below them, or maybe run, stumbling in the furrows just to hurry and have it over. But that was always a mistake because the clatter only got louder and made you feel you might go crazy if it didn't stop.

At one time Alberta had been afraid of the cornfield, afraid she would get lost and start going in circles and would finally just crouch down and die because she couldn't stand the leaves grabbing her any more or the maddening noise in her ears. Then one time she did get lost, and heard her own voice speaking in her head, "Just follow the furrows. You can't help but come out at one end or the other."

After that she wasn't afraid in the cornfield much and even liked its dark jungleness and she thought maybe she would bring her cowboy party out here to play some kind of wild, spooky hide-and-seek. She would only have to make sure they didn't knock down any corn stalks when they got to running and screaming.

She walked, crouched and keen-eyed, and at a certain point veered off to the right, seeing if she could cut across the furrows and come out at the ditch where there was a plank across to the back yard. But after going a ways she didn't see daylight shining through the corn rows like she expected to. So she started following the furrows straight, not knowing where she would come out now.

When she did see the light again she hurried toward it, then froze because she had come out not on their side of the field but on Rexleys' side, right behind Rexleys' barn. And there in his hat the color of a dead mouse was Old Man Rexley pouring something brown from a whiskey bottle into a ditch. Quietly she tried to edge back into the cornfield but a leaf rustled. Old Man Rexley looked up and saw her from under his old brown hat.

They looked at each other a long time and finally Old Man Rexley seemed to grin. He held up the bottle for her to see and said in a normal old man's voice, "Whiskey. I'm just rinsing out the bottle."

"I thought you couldn't hear," she said.

"I can't very well," he said. "Although I'm better out in the air."

"Ione said you couldn't talk anymore."

"Well sometimes I have a good day."

"She said you haven't talked for a year."

"This is my first good day for a long time. Sometimes they say that happens right before the end. I don't expect to last much longer."

She stood still watching him.

"What you saw me doing just now," Old Man Rexley said, "was rinsing out the bottle. After I drink all the whiskey I come down and rinse out the bottle."

"It looked like you were pouring all the whiskey out," she said.

"No. I was rinsing it."

"Why?"

"Ione don't like the smell of liquor so I rinse it out of the bottles."

"Why not rinse it in the sink?"

"Well. She says it stinks up her sink."

"Why not rinse it with the hose?"

"Oh Johnny took the hose off somewhere."

She stood watching him for a minute. He seemed like an entirely different person from the near-dead old man who sat in the shadows of Ione's living room. Finally she said, "It looked to me like you were pouring brown whiskey in the ditch."

"Say," Old Man Rexley said. "Here's a dime." He fished in his pants pocket and found something he held out but she wouldn't have reached across to him for the world.

"Look here," Old Man Rexley said, "You're trespassing on my property. But don't say nothing and we'll just forget about it. Else I'll have to call the sheriff."

"I'm on our side of the ditch," she said. "Don't be silly."

Old Man Rexley turned and looked back toward his own barnyard.

"I did just pour out this bottle," he turned back around and said. "I usually drink it. But today I wasn't feeling good so I came and poured it out."

"I thought you were having a good day."

"I am when it comes to talking. But my stomach's acting up. It just don't want to hold a thing." Old Man Rexley put his fist on his stomach to show where it hurt.

"Why didn't you save it for tomorrow?"

"It doesn't keep good," Old Man Rexley said. "In this hot weather."

Alberta didn't know whether liquor kept or not, once it had been opened. Old Man Rexley said, "That's why I'm asking you not to tell anybody you saw me pouring it out."

"Why?"

"Well because I'd hate Ione to know I'm wasting her milk money like this."

"She would probably rather you poured it out than

drank it."

"Well," Old Man Rexley said. "She might if it didn't cost so much."

"How much does it cost?"

"Five dollars," Old Man Rexley said, and Alberta whistled.

"So that's why I don't want you to tell anybody," he said. "Now here's the dime."

But she didn't want to reach her hand out to him.

"You're not going to tell anybody now," Old Man Rexley said, in the same tone as if she'd taken the dime.

Alberta shrugged.

"Ione'll give me heck," Old Man Rexley said. "Now promise me you won't tell her. I'm going to die soon anyhow so I don't want her giving me heck right here at the end."

Finally Alberta said OK she promised.

He turned and she watched him wade back through the weeds from the ditch bank to his own barnyard, his old hat pulled low and the whiskey bottle half hidden under his arm. When he was gone she followed along the ditch until it came to their place, then on farther to the plank where you could cross into the back yard.

Here the sheets were still up on the clotheslines, dry now and sharp in the sunlight, making white hallways across the back yard and she walked through them, as if between the walls of a mansion.

It was odd how they could live right next to the Rexleys and be nothing at all like them.

Grandma was out digging in her rose bushes as if not noticing Mama's sheets taking over the whole back yard. It was a lesson as to what Grandma would and wouldn't dare to do.

When Alberta came up Grandma stopped digging and wiped the back of her neck with a handkerchief, then asked Alberta if she wanted to ride with her up to Uncle Edmund's mine in Sparta about two hours away.

She didn't much want to go to Uncle Edmund's but Grandma said they would stop in Bonner on the way and have iced tea or a coke at The Fountain.

"What are you going to tell him?" Alberta asked.

"Why that we feel sorry for Adelaide but that of course the plot was meant for real family."

Alberta was tired and had been dreading the walk back down to the field with the full gallon of water, damp and clanking with ice, so she said she would go if Grandma would drive her down with the water. They made a deal and Alberta went up over the cellar to change into a clean shirt.

In a few minutes they met in the barnyard, Grandma in a different dress with her handbag clamped under her elbow and a spot of rouge on each cheek.

They got into Grandma's hot old car and drove down the lane to the hay stack, Grandma humming as she always did when she drove, interrupting herself to mutter things toward dogs that ran out or to ask a quick question, "What's Stanton got that baler parked there for?" then humming again, not expecting you to answer. When they passed George McKay, coming up the lane from his place on his big putt-putting John Deere tractor she nodded her head in a way Alberta thought was silly and embarrassing, and muttered, "Hello, how are you? Dum-de-dum," as if he could read her lips. George McKay lifted one finger off the steering wheel as they passed, which was the way most men waved when they were driving, never smiling, lifting that one finger the same to everybody, whether you were driving in the car with the whole family or it was just you on your bicycle.

After they left the water at the stack, Alberta nestling it under the hay on the shady side and making sure Junior saw, they drove back up the lane, then up the cemetery road to town, Grandma stopping at the stop sign by the store, though most people didn't bother. They went up the main street of Adair, past the store and the two pool halls and then turned at what had been a movie house for about six months, but which had been turned into the Grange Hall. Behind the Grange Hall was the new trailer court Bookers had made out of the front half of their cow pasture. Nobody knew where the trailer court people were coming from, but now there were five trailers and one of the girls who lived there was in Alberta's baton twirling class. Once Alberta had ridden her bicycle through the trailer court fast and now, since it was a day for strangeness, she said to Grandma, "Let's drive through and have a look," but Grandma didn't pay attention.

Then they were out of town, past the high school and the football field and winding up through the dry brown slopes on the valley's edge that people called Dry Gulch. The Dry Gulch people only had the right to use water after the main valley people finished irrigating. Lots of times, like right now in the hottest part of the summer, there wasn't any water to spare for Dry Gulch and the people out here had to let their pastures bake in the sun.

"I bet it makes them mad they have to let us take all the water first," Alberta remarked as they drove through Dry Gulch where it seemed twice as hot as at home. If you stopped the car out here you could hear the weeds popping by the side of the road, snapping like Rice Krispies as they exploded in the heat. The bugs buzzed like they were being fried in a pan.

The people who lived out here always seemed a little different, quiet and staring. It was like being out here in the dry hills they nearly forgot how to talk.

"Don't you think it makes them mad?" Alberta asked.

"I suppose," Grandma said. "What?"

She couldn't carry on a conversation when she drove and only halfway heard what you said. If you said something or even told her a whole long thing while she was driving, she would only faintly remember it later.

Now the road dropped down again and fell in alongside Powder River and they started on the winding ride through the canyon, following the twists of the river. It was a road that always made you feel sick because of so many curves, and you were always nervous because of the logging trucks that came roaring around the curves, sometimes taking up half your lane. Driving with Dad, who went too fast and would take long looks at you just as a curve was coming up, Alberta had to keep her eyes glued to the road. Even so, she often dreamt of Dad in his pickup, flying out over the river canyon, still grinning and joking with the gas jammed clear to the floor.

But now she could relax since Grandma drove slow and gripped the wheel like they were facing death all the way, breaking into a hum at the most dangerous times, as when a truck roared out from behind a curve.

"Remember that time your papa got buried under the snow?" Alberta asked suddenly.

"Snow?" Grandma said, and frowned a little, but then her face straightened out since she couldn't think very far into things while she was driving. Alberta hoped in this way to plant ideas in her mind. Then, if Grandma should ever hear Alberta had told about Thomas Pratt buried under the snow, Grandma might say, "Well, I do seem to remember hearing something like that."

"He just had a few matches and a New Testament and some jerky," Alberta said.

"Fiddlesticks," Grandma said, but in an absent-minded way like somebody trying to read and answer you at the same time.

"He kept himself busy memorizing the New Testament."

"Of course he knew his Scripture," Grandma said, and Alberta smiled out the window at how easy you could trick her with anything religious.

They drove along the well-known road, past the big white rock which was half way to Bonner, past

Immigrant Springs where you could stop and drink water bubbling from a pipe in the ground, past a little green shack which was all that was left of the hotel where people used to stay when it took two days to get to Bonner in a horse and wagon. When Grandma was a little girl she never got to go to Bonner. Only Thomas Pratt got to go, staying away several days, then coming home with six months of store-bought supplies in the back of the wagon. Grandma would look at the sacks of flour and sugar, Alberta imagined, and try to tell from them what Bonner was like. It seemed a shame Thomas Pratt never took her once.

"I'm going to Alabama with Martha Lee when she goes," Alberta said, to see how much attention Grandma really could pay. "We're going to airline stewardess school."

But standing in the road was a deer, its head turned to gaze right at them, and Grandma started to hum, pumping the brakes and reaching out her arm to hold Alberta against the seat. They rolled to a stop a few inches from the deer who stood without budging, gazing with big distant brown eyes that looked a little like Mama's.

Grandma blew the horn and banged on the outside of the door, but it was a minute or two before the deer turned its long neck up towards the sagebrush foothill as if trying to remember something, then finally, without giving them any last look, went jumping up it like a rabbit.

"Deer never used to come down and stand in the road like that," Grandma said. "They used to stay up in the hills where they belonged."

When they got to Bonner, Grandma had to go to the courthouse on some business and she let Alberta off to walk on First Street under the striped canvas awnings the stores had for shade.

Bonner was the county seat with a population of 9,354

and they went there twice a month to shop and go to the dentist or do other business. Alberta knew the town well, and had spent hours and hours walking up and down First Street. She was completely familiar with each store, from the dime store to the 88-cent store to the stationery store by the Geyser Grand Hotel where the bus stopped.

At Christmas time, Bonner seemed too hectic as you ran from one store to the other, cold outside, hot inside, trying to compare the different things, knowing you had to decide fast before time to go home. Or, when you were visiting the dentist, the town was sickening and you hated the candy smells in the dime store and the frying that came from the restaurants. But on a summer day like this with no appointment or presents to buy, it was a chance to watch how the town people, especially the men, clean and hatless, big-bellied in their slacks and short-sleeve shirts, would stand talking under the awnings, as if they were in their own yards. You could tell they all worked in stores by their soft whiteness and by the little white plastic pockets they wore inside their regular shirt pockets to hook their ball point pens to. They seemed another thing altogether from the farmers going by in their pickups. Here in town, even in their good hats, the farmers looked skinny and tight, their skin burned and dried to red ash. While the town men seemed plump and cool as grapes, or like they were all preachers or big human cats, not exactly men at all.

After walking by all the stores and going into the dime stores and the 88-cent store, Alberta walked down to the Geyser Grand Hotel where anybody could use the bathroom and get a drink since that was where the bus stopped.

The Geyser Grand Hotel was the biggest building in Bonner, three stories high and bright mustard color with big curlicues on each corner. But inside it was dark and ugly with the smell of buses. A dozen old men sat still as death in cracked green chairs, and in the bathroom all of the toilets but one were locked, so you had to pay a dime to use them. It was so you wouldn't catch anything from the people coming through on the bus and Grandma always spent the dime even if the free toilet was vacant.

Alone Alberta crawled under the door to get to the clean toilet, just hoping the bus people hadn't thought of doing the same.

Back out in the lobby one of the old men in the chairs gave her a fishy look and said something she didn't get. She hurried out thinking of Mama here alone among the nasty old men, the time she had come to catch the bus and leave. Maybe she had only come back home because the Geyser Grand was so awful that she couldn't bear to wait for the bus. But that was before an airliner landed in Bonner.

She went back up the street to meet Grandma in front of The Fountain. Grandma was already there waiting, standing stiffly on the corner in the sun, looking up and down in a jerky way, her handbag clutched under her elbow. When Alberta got there they went inside where it was cooled with fans and sat down in a white painted booth by the plate glass window so they could still watch everybody walking by. Grandma had iced tea and Alberta had a coke, and Grandma put her money out on the table as if to prove she had enough although of course you didn't pay until later.

Whenever Grandma was out in public she did everything too soon or too fast and so in comparison Alberta tried to do things very slowly, and now would only sip her coke without even picking it up. Whereas Grandma fidgeted with her tea, twisting and shredding her little piece of lemon until it looked like a rag. And where Grandma nodded and murmured at everybody who walked by, whether they even seemed to be looking in the window, tapping all the time on the table with her fingers, Alberta sat still and looked at everybody coldly.

"Well," Grandma said when they had cooled off. "I looked Adelaide up in the court house. She is one of the Burnt River Bairds."

Grandma fixed Alberta with a stare, though she had never heard of any Burnt River Bairds.

"Sylvan Lacey's wife Alveda is a Baird," Grandma said.

Alberta knew Alveda well. In church on Christmas she always sang "Star of the East" as a solo and everybody gritted their teeth when she tried to hit the high note. Other than that she was nice, smiling so much her eyes almost disappeared. "That doesn't make Adelaide a Lacey," Alberta said. "Anymore than it makes her one of us."

"The Laceys suck everybody and everything into themselves," Grandma said. "They would suck up this whole country if somebody didn't stop them."

"Oh well," Alberta said. "You weren't going to let her in anyway."

"Laceys filling up Papa's cemetery," Grandma said, looking out the window at the Bonner people.

"Yeah and they fill up his church too," Alberta said. "At Easter and Christmas. I bet they'll even be filling up heaven when you get there."

Grandma gave Alberta a hard look and said, "I know your mother thinks it's smart to say so."

"Well, won't they all go to heaven if they go to church?" Alberta asked, slightly embarrassed to be caught repeating Mama.

Grandma opened her handbag and took out her handkerchief to wipe her lips, even though there were paper napkins. Then she snapped her handbag shut and went over to pay, leaving Alberta to suck up the last drops of coke.

They went out onto the street that seemed baking now and walked to the hot stuffy car which Grandma started with a roar, pulling the hand brake loose with a fierce jerk.

They drove back through Bonner and got onto the cracked old road that led up to Sparta where once thousands of Chinese and white men had mined for gold. Now Sparta was a ghost town with only two or three old men like Uncle Edmund still trying to mine.

After a while the cracked pavement gave out and they were driving on gravel and dirt, stirring up a huge cloud of dust that would choke anybody coming behind.

It was not a dangerous road, since it didn't go along a river canyon. It was only a slow dusty climb with nothing to see but the brown sagebrush hills spread out all around like rumpled bed covers. As they rode Alberta practiced her party stories on Grandma, telling first about the murderer with the hook for the hand, then about the guy, without giving him a name, who had gotten caught in the blizzard and had to cut his horse open and get into the hot steamy insides to survive.

"Finally he had to cut out the raw horse liver and eat it," Alberta said as a wrap-up.

"Law," Grandma said, not really hearing, and Alberta considered telling her about the breasts like bullets but, glancing sideways at Grandma's stiff profile, didn't.

They got up to Sparta which was now just a long double row of falling-down shacks stretching out a ways before the sagebrush started in again. Behind the street ran the creek where the miners had found gold.

Most of the buildings had only been shacks, even when they were new and standing upright. The only good building on a stone foundation had been the dance hall and it still stood, its double doors boarded shut.

There hadn't been a single church and Grandma said, "I expect that's why it all fell down."

Uncle Edmund's shack, at the end of the street, looked about the same as all the others, although when you got close you could see a few yellow boards nailed on to the old gray ones where he had tried to fix it up. From a ways away they could see Uncle Edmund sitting out on the porch in a straight-back rocking chair. As they drove up he leaned forward to spit over the railing and then stood, wobbling a little on his broken ankles and looking at them with his crafty eyes so you couldn't tell whether they'd surprised him or not.

"By golly," he yelled when they were getting out of the car. "You're just in time."

"For what?" Alberta called back, afraid they would have to try to eat his stew as they had on another visit. It had been so gray and funny-looking neither one of them could touch it and Grandma had told a lie and said they'd both just had hamburgers and milkshakes in Bonner.

But he never said what they were in time for and when they were inside his shack, with its funny smell and picture calendars everywhere, though none with the right month or year, he didn't try to give them anything to eat. He just sat down on the chair he'd brought in from the porch, leaning over to spit in the can that was already there waiting.

"Say," Uncle Edmund said after they'd been there a minute with Grandma still fluttery and polite and not yet ready to say what she'd come for. "Here's something to see." He got up and wobbled over to a cupboard and came back with the mustard jar he always showed you when you came. It had all his gold in it, little brownish yellow rocks that looked kind of like pieces of scrambled egg.

"Do you have any new ones in here?" Alberta asked, wondering what one of the little nuggets was worth and whether she could somehow get one to show Martha Lee. There was one nugget she always especially admired, round with six little points that made it look like a picture of the sun. In the center of it were three little cracks that made a kind of face, and you could see it made into a beautiful necklace. It was the biggest one and the one Uncle Edmund always kept on top. She knew, if she wanted to get a nugget somehow, she had to do it before Grandma told him about the cemetery. But she couldn't ask him to give her one and it seemed too rude to ask what one might cost.

"Sure there's new ones," Uncle Edmund said, looking all around so you didn't believe him.

"How's Adelaide?" Grandma asked, still holding her handbag tight under her elbow. "And her family," she added dangerously.

"Say," Uncle Edmund said. "Would you folks like a bite to eat?"

Grandma said no thank you they couldn't stay but a minute. That they'd had to go to Bonner and just thought they'd run on up here but they couldn't stay.

Alberta got up to put the mustard jar back.

But Grandma kept sitting politely, clasping her handbag under her elbow. Uncle Edmund got up and started to walk around the kitchen, first pouring water from a five gallon can into a pot and then lighting his kerosene stove and fishing some tea bags out of a paper sack he found on one of his shelves. They both watched him closely as he got two cups and a glass down from another shelf and sat them in his wash basin, then poured water from the can over them as a rinse. He gave them a crafty look to show he knew they were watching him like hawks.

When the tea was ready they both drank politely and said it hit the spot, even though it wasn't very hot and had a funny vegetably taste.

Now it seemed Grandma had to wait until she drank his tea to tell him Adelaide wasn't getting in the cemetery and so they all sat sipping. Grandma though seemed to be getting over her politeness. She had stopped smiling in her nervous visiting way and grew stiffer every minute.

"Speaking of Bonner," Uncle Edmund said, looking craftily toward Grandma. "Remember when they brought the liberty bell on a flatcar to Bonner, Lucille. Nineteen seventeen or eighteen."

"Nineteen eighteen," Grandma said stiffly.

"The real liberty bell with the crack?" Alberta asked.

"Yessir," Uncle Edmund said. "Hauled it out on a flatcar. Me and your grandma went to Bonner in a buggy with some beau of hers to see it. We had a good time that day didn't we Lucille?"

Grandma held her tea cup on her knee and looked into the distance.

"Remember that Lucille?" Uncle Edmund said. "Everybody got in to Bonner somehow. Horseback, wagon and team, pony cart. A few people even had motor cars by then."

"Cease Gillette had that White Steamer."

"Oh that White Steamer," Uncle Edmund cried. "By golly that was some rig. Remember how he'd take people for rides? He'd take a whole load from the store in Adair down the road to the cemetery and back."

But he had mentioned the wrong word and Grandma said stiffly, "People get to the cemetery the best way they can I suppose."

"Now that car would carry seven passengers," Uncle Edmund went on. "Then when he'd get as many as he could stuffed inside he'd put a couple of cowboys out to lay across the radiator. And some more on the running boards. Remember that Lucille? Them going down the road thataway?"

"Yes," Grandma said. "I remember those crazy boys."

"Scared the horses with that car," Uncle Edmund said. "People got mad. One fella over in Six Mile tried to make a law not to let cars come in the valley at all because of the menace to livestock."

Grandma's mouth twitched a little toward a smile and Uncle Edmund leaned toward her.

"Remember Alice Blunt?" he said. "Somehow she got her a car."

"I know how she got it," Grandma said. "Selling magazine subscriptions. She'd come and wouldn't leave until you bought one. Then she got the car," Grandma spoke now to Alberta, "and her father wouldn't let her drive it because it wasn't ladylike."

"Oh that went out pretty quick," Uncle Edmund said. "It wasn't long after that she was driving it because I remember that time the dog ran out in front of her and she hit him. Right by the high school."

Grandma put her hand over her mouth to cover a smile. Uncle Edmund leaned toward her.

"She couldn't bear for the poor animal to suffer," he said. "So to put him out of his misery she was gonna beat him to death with her umbrella. But as soon as she swung at him he got up and ran off."

Grandma laughed outright, letting her handbag slip, and Uncle Edmund sat back, his one old blue eye suddenly open and blazing.

"Those was times," Uncle Edmund said. "We were young and cars was just starting to come in."

"Yes that's true," Grandma said. "It seemed like lots was happening."

"Now though," Uncle Edmund said. "I wish it hadn't."

Alberta got up to look at the mustard jar of gold some more since it didn't seem like they were leaving right away and in the pause said, "Have you looked any more for that vein of gold you and Greatgrandpa found up here somewhere?"

"Fiddlesticks," Grandma said. She leaned over to pick up her handbag from where it had slipped onto the floor. "They cleaned out what little gold was here sixty years ago. They didn't leave a crumb."

"By golly I'll show you a crumb," Uncle Edmund said. He got up and wobbled out the back door on his weak ankles and left the door open so they could hear the creek going by.

They didn't speak, waiting for him to come back. Alberta studied his calendars which all came from 1951. That must have been the year he came to live here and wanted to decorate. He had turned the pages clear to December on some of them. Others he had left in the summer, like one with a picture of flowers blooming in front of mountains and an advertisement for the Bonner drugstore. After she'd looked at them all she went over to his cot and pulled back the edge of the army blanket to see if he used sheets. She was surprised to see the sheets bright and white, then remembered Adelaide.

"Why don't you tell him?"

"When he comes back."

But he didn't come back so they finally went out the door and down to the creek and a ways off they saw Uncle Edmund crouching by the creek rinsing a gold pan of dirt in the flowing water. When he saw them Uncle Edmund said, "I'll tell you how much gold there was. See that pile. What do you think that is?"

He pointed with his shaking old finger to a stack of boulders across the creek.

Grandma stared across the creek and didn't speak.

"Someplace they found gold?" Alberta guessed.

"Nosir," Uncle Edmund said. "That's the old cemetery. Now why do you think it's up there?"

"Because this was a wicked town and it was the best they deserved," Grandma said.

"Nosir," Uncle Edmund said. "I'll tell you why. When the first man died up here they went to dig him a nice grave by the creek. And before they got it dug they hit bedrock and got sixteen dollars worth of gold in the first pan. So they said, 'Say, let's not waste any good dirt,' and they moved him to a rock pile."

"Well I'm glad you have such a nice cemetery," Grandma said, her arms clamped to her chest, but Uncle Edmund was back working with his pan, dipping and swirling, always shaking a little so any gold would keep settled to the bottom while the dirt washed off.

"Sure they had a cemetery," Uncle Edmund said, sitting back on his heels and putting the gold pan down. All you could see in it so far was mud. "For the white men. Of course you know what they did for the Chinee men."

He looked up craftily from his squat.

"I expect they had their own cemetery," Grandma said.

"Sure they did," Uncle Edmund said. "In the bottom of the mine."

"Edmund, hush."

"Come pay day...," Uncle Edmund began.

"We can only stay a minute," Grandma said. "Alberta run get my handkerchief I left in the car."

But Grandma's handkerchief was poking out of her bosom where she kept it.

"Come pay day what," Alberta asked.

"Come pay day," Uncle Edmund said, "they'd flood the mine. Before they had to pay up. Then there the Chinee men was, already buried."

"They did no such thing," Grandma said.

"The heck they didn't," Uncle Edmund said. "Those was tough times. And my dad was right in the middle of it."

"He never had anything to do with the mines or miners," Grandma said. "Of course."

"I guess he didn't find that vein of gold," Uncle Edmund said. "I guess he didn't dig right into her and say, 'Why here's a vein as big as your arm.'"

"Then why couldn't you ever find it?" Alberta ask.

"That's right," Grandma said. "There isn't a crumb of gold left in this whole country."

"By golly I'll show you a crumb," Uncle Edmund said, and he started washing his gold pan again. "This is dirt I brought down just yesterday from a vein I'm working. It's not the same kind of vein my dad and I found that time. This here's not so big but I'll show you something anyhow."

"Papa never kited around the hills looking for gold," Grandma said. "He stayed right at home building up the place. Then when he'd done that he built the church."

"The heck he didn't," Uncle Edmund said, still dipping and swirling. "He found that vein and was gonna go back but then he got sick. 'Edmund remember that vein of gold,' he said and those was his last words."

"In his last words he accepted Jesus," Alberta said. She looked at Grandma who said, "Of course he did."

Uncle Edmund got up and aimed his eye at Grandma, his shaking old finger pointed at her chest.

"I'll tell you what his last words were." Uncle Edmund held Grandma silent with his finger. "I know because I was right there when he died. I can see him plain as I'm looking at you."

"His last words. . . ," Alberta began, wondering why Grandma didn't speak up.

"I'll tell you his last words," Uncle Edmund interrupted, his old eye glued to Grandma who stared back, her mouth clamped. "He said, 'Find that gold,' and he waved his hand like this."

Uncle Edmund passed the palm of his old hand slowly in front of his face.

"And then I'll tell you what he did," Uncle Edmund said. "He slumped his head down like this and died."

Uncle Edmund let his head fall down on his chest and neither of them spoke until he lifted it up to spit behind him into the creek.

"If he said, 'Find the gold,' Grandma said, her voice shaking, "he was talking about heaven."

"Weren't you there?" Alberta asked.

"I was right beside his chair, Alberta," Grandma said in a hard voice. "That blue chair."

"Then why did you say, '*If* he said....'"

"I can tell you what he said," Uncle Edmund said. "No ifs ands or buts."

"He said, 'Jesus forgive me for my sins,'" Grandma said, her eyes black.

"Horse manure," Uncle Edmund said. "He never had any use for Jesus living or dying. He could take care of himself, by God." Uncle Edmund turned his back on them, wobbling off down the creek.

"Alberta," Grandma said, spinning around to walk back through the house. "Get in the car."

But Alberta didn't follow.

Out front Grandma started the car with a roar but Alberta ignored it. She picked up the gold pan Uncle Edmund had left and started to dip and swirl, dip and swirl. She and Martha Lee would get a tent and come up here and camp, mining all day and getting enough money to fly around the world.

She dipped and swirled, making the black dirt lacy on the side of the pan like you were supposed to and before very long she saw a bright gleam from the wet dirt, a nugget, a big one. In fact it was the same sun-looking nugget with the smiling face. She saw that Uncle Edmund had slipped it into the pan so he could pretend he'd found gold.

She picked the nugget out and washed it in the creek and looked at it glowing wetly. It would serve him right if she just stole it, but she would rather have him know she'd found out his trick so she took the nugget back and put it in the mustard jar.

It was kind of a relief to know anything anybody said was just a story.

Then there was nothing to do but go out and get in the car with Grandma.

They drove home in silence, Grandma not humming, even when they almost ran over a jack rabbit. Alberta slouched against the hot fuzzy seat, letting her legs spraddle apart the way Grandma hated.

Halfway home Grandma said, "I'll have to write him a letter I guess about the cemetery," but Alberta did not reply. If she were Adelaide she wouldn't touch that cemetery with a ten-foot pole.

At home the confusion was over, the sheets back on the beds, the curtains hung and the floors shining with new wax. The living room, so sad and bare this morning, now seemed to glow in a golden light, reflecting the vases of yellow roses from out by the gate. Alberta's own room had entirely changed, with all her things out of sight, stuffed in one half of the closet. The other half was left empty for Aunt Rae. There were roses here too and an embroidered white bedspread Alberta had never seen. The curtains were starched and had lost the folds of dust which you could watch as you lay in bed until you saw faces and other pictures.

In the dining room Mama had taken all her wedding dishes out of the glass cabinet and stacked them on the table and had lined up the glasses on the buffet. The dishes were a cream color and the glasses all stood up on a narrow stem. Both were circled by a narrow band of gold.

On the davenport sat the wooden chest with the red velvet lining which held the wedding silverware. Mama was wiping each dish in case it had gotten dusty in the cabinet and Alberta got the silver polish and a rag to do the silverware. While they wiped they tried to think when they had used the wedding dishes and the glasses last and finally decided it had been Thanksgiving two years ago when Uncle Edmund, Joanne and her French boyfriend Gilbert had all come to dinner. It was the French boyfriend that had made them feel like being so fancy.

Sometimes they used the wedding dishes for Christmas. But the glasses, or the crystal Mama called it, had never been used that Alberta could remember. Mama said, Oh surely they had been, but neither could remember when.

"I know I've used them," Mama said, "because one of the parfait glasses got broken."

She pointed out which ones were the parfait glasses, the ones shaped kind of like an egg. Then Alberta had a distant memory of seeing a dessert in them, green and white in layers. That made Mama remember making a dessert once when there were still enough women in the valley to have bridge club. Then two of the women who played bridge had moved away and so there weren't enough to make two tables. And it had just not seemed like an evening, Mama said, with only one table.

They'd never used any of the other glasses, the big water glasses, the wine glasses, or the little tiny eight-sided glasses which even Mama couldn't remember exactly what they were for. But when Aunt Rae and Martha Lee were here, they would try to use them all.

Alberta asked when they were first going to use the china and crystal and Mama said breakfast.

"Breakfast?"

"We're going to have creamed beef on toast and orange juice in these." She held up the ones that were really for wine.

"For breakfast?"

"You can have a nice meal at breakfast," Mama said. "You don't have to have the same thing every day."

"What did you have at home for breakfast," Alberta asked after polishing a while.

"Nothing particular."

"What do you mean nothing particular?"

"You had whatever the maid cooked that morning."

"Like what?"

"Scrambled eggs. Fish sometimes. Hush puppies."

"What did you drink?"

"Oh, milk. Or cocoa."

"The maid fixed everything and brought it to you?"

"Yes."

"Did you help her do the dishes?"

"No. Sometimes I went and talked to her while she was doing them."

Alberta polished the silver, marveling at the hidden magic of this past life which Mama hardly ever mentioned.

She asked, "What will we have for breakfast after the first day?"

"We'll have to see what they like."

"Will we keep having breakfast on the wedding dishes?"

Mama thought and said yes, she thought they would use only the wedding dishes while the company was here and just be very careful.

"Will we use the crystal all the time too?"

"Just at supper maybe."

Alberta finished with the knives and forks and spoons, and turned to the cute little salad forks, then the big boat-like serving spoons. Last she did the tiny little forks that were to spear things like pickles and olives so you wouldn't have to pick them up with your fingers.

She said, "Will Martha Lee go to baton lessons with me?"

"Maybe," Mama said. "That's a good idea."

"Do you think she's had any lessons?"

"In Japan? I'd be surprised."

"What if she's scared sleeping up over the cellar."

"That's the only bed we've got for her so she better not be."

"Do you think she'll like it here?"

"Probably."

"Do you think Aunt Rae will like it?"

Mama was getting tired of talking and nodded yes.

"Do you think I'll live here when I grow up?"

"I don't know," Mama said.

"Where then," Alberta quickly asked. "Alabama?"

"No."

"Where then? Guess. Guess."

But Mama said she didn't have any idea and couldn't guess and she saw she had to take all the crystal in the kitchen to wash it after all since it had a film of dust she couldn't wipe off. Alberta should very carefully put the good dishes back on the shelf and then why didn't she go practice her baton now that they thought of it.

"If you had been practicing better," Mama said, "you could have put on a show in the yard after dark."

Alberta felt stabbed. Oh why hadn't she been practicing her baton the way she should have? She could have had everybody line up in chairs out in the yard. Mama could have put the record player in the doorway and put on the baton music, "Muskrat Ramble." Then Alberta could have come marching out in shorts and her high white boots with her baton that had batteries so it lit up blue on one end and red on the other.

What if she had practiced and gotten really good and could have performed in the yard with them all watching?

The baton lessons were Mama's idea. Grandma was against it. She was against the coach's wife who taught it, who had come from California and wore an ankle bracelet. And she was against the other girls in the class, two of them from the trailer court. She had a fit when she heard their plan to twirl at the high school football games, strutting out on the football field in short green skirts and green satin panties.

"Of course you will not do that," Grandma had said, "with girls from the trailer court or any other way. What is your mother thinking?"

"If your class twirls at the football game you will too," Mama had said with surprising force. And to prove it she had ordered an expensive pair of white majorette boots from the coach's wife's catalog.

Baton lessons seemed to be one of those odd places where Mama wouldn't give up.

Mama could say, If she doesn't march with the baton class, I'm leaving.

Then Grandma would get Dad out in the barnyard. They would stand talking, her arms crossed, her skirt whipping.

She will not march with those trailer court girls, Grandma would say. Dad would throw down his hat and stomp on it. But he would remember whose farm it was. Finally he would have to do what she said and tell Alberta, You can't march out there with your panties showing.

Mama would pack and leave, this time going out to the airport where it was more pleasant. She would fly to Alabama and when she landed there would be her aunts and maids, waving and saying, Lucky you finally made it. Within a day or two, Oregon would disappear as far as she was concerned.

Alberta would still be there with no mother or baton class either and Dad dropped into silence.

Then she might set fire to the house herself.

So maybe it would be good to give up baton right now.

But you couldn't tell what would lead to what. You couldn't give up everything just in case.

So she went out to practice in the barnyard where Grandma couldn't see. She took the kitchen timer so she could follow the instructions Mama had written on a big piece of cardboard: figure eights for ten minutes, cross-hand twirl for ten minutes, finger twirl for ten minutes. Then she practiced pitching for five minutes. Finally, for as long as she could, she was supposed to hum "Muskrat Ramble" and practice strutting with her baton under her arm. It was how they would walk out on the football field but Mama said Alberta didn't strut right.

She didn't really know what they meant by strut and once Mama had tried to show her. She had put the baton under her arm and tried to strut but she didn't do it right either. Her bottom looked too big as it waved back and forth and Alberta was glad when she stopped, nervous that Grandma might come around the corner of the house.

In fact, it seemed nobody knew what was meant by strutting. All five girls did something different and they looked stupid following each other around the coach's wife's yard. The coach's wife looked stupid too, leaning way back and twitching her bottom in a way Alberta wouldn't want to do if she could.

It seemed they should just forget strutting and march,

not trying to lean back or wiggle in any special way.

Then on the Fourth of July they had gone to the fire works in Bonner and saw the Elks Drum and Bugle Corps and the baton twirler who led them out onto the field. She had on white boots and a skintight bathing suit covered with glitter and she twirled two flaming batons at the same time, jumping and dancing and kicking out her legs. Watching her lead the drum and bugle corps, Alberta saw how you were supposed to strut, leaning back but just a little and somehow making your legs stretch out long in front of you, not twitching or wiggling just somehow—but you couldn't say exactly what it was, even having seen it.

So then Alberta had tried to practice more. She had tried to think of herself as that Elk's baton twirler.

"That's it," Mama had yelled once when she walked by and saw her practicing.

"What?"

"That's how to strut. Do it again."

But she couldn't remember what she had done and hadn't ever been able to do it again. It had just come once for a second and then was gone.

Still it seemed she might hit on strutting again and maybe would hit on twirling the same way. Maybe she would hit on it before the company came.

She put the dishes carefully in the cabinet with the glass doors. Now she was anxious to go practice her baton, so Mama said, OK, go ahead but put on your tennis shoes and don't get your feet all green from the grass.

In fact, Mama said, try hard to keep clean because with only one bathroom and the extra people, we can't all take baths all the time. And, though Alberta often took baths in Grandma's, just for a change, Mama said not to take one in there while the company was here. It might give Grandma something to blame on them. Also, Mama said, never take Martha Lee to Grandma's house unless they were specifically invited, and don't play on her side of the yard too much.

But Alberta felt too disgusted with Grandma to even let her get a glimpse of Martha Lee.

She got her baton and the piece of cardboard with the instructions on it and the kitchen timer and went out to the barnyard, to the one grassy part in the middle where no cars or trucks drove, neither the ones going to the house nor the ones going to the barn.

It was late afternoon now, and the barnyard was in shade, the shadow of the house long and pointed, and the shadow from the big tree completely blotting out the far half of the yard. Behind her the barn rose up, its unpainted boards sucking up the last red sun. She set the timer and propped the cardboard up with a stick, then began doing figure eights. But the figure eights were too easy and weren't pretty so she went to the cross-hand twirl. But that was easy too, and she saw that she knew how to do all the twirls just standing there, but what made a good show like the Elks twirler was to jump and dance around while you were twirling. So she tried to jump and dance around while doing the figure eights and cross-hand twirl. Maybe if she imagined herself as the Elks twirler, as she had the other time, it would come. But it didn't and she couldn't think which way to jump or how to dance. The sun got so low the shade from the big tree blotted out the whole barnyard but still nothing inside opened up.

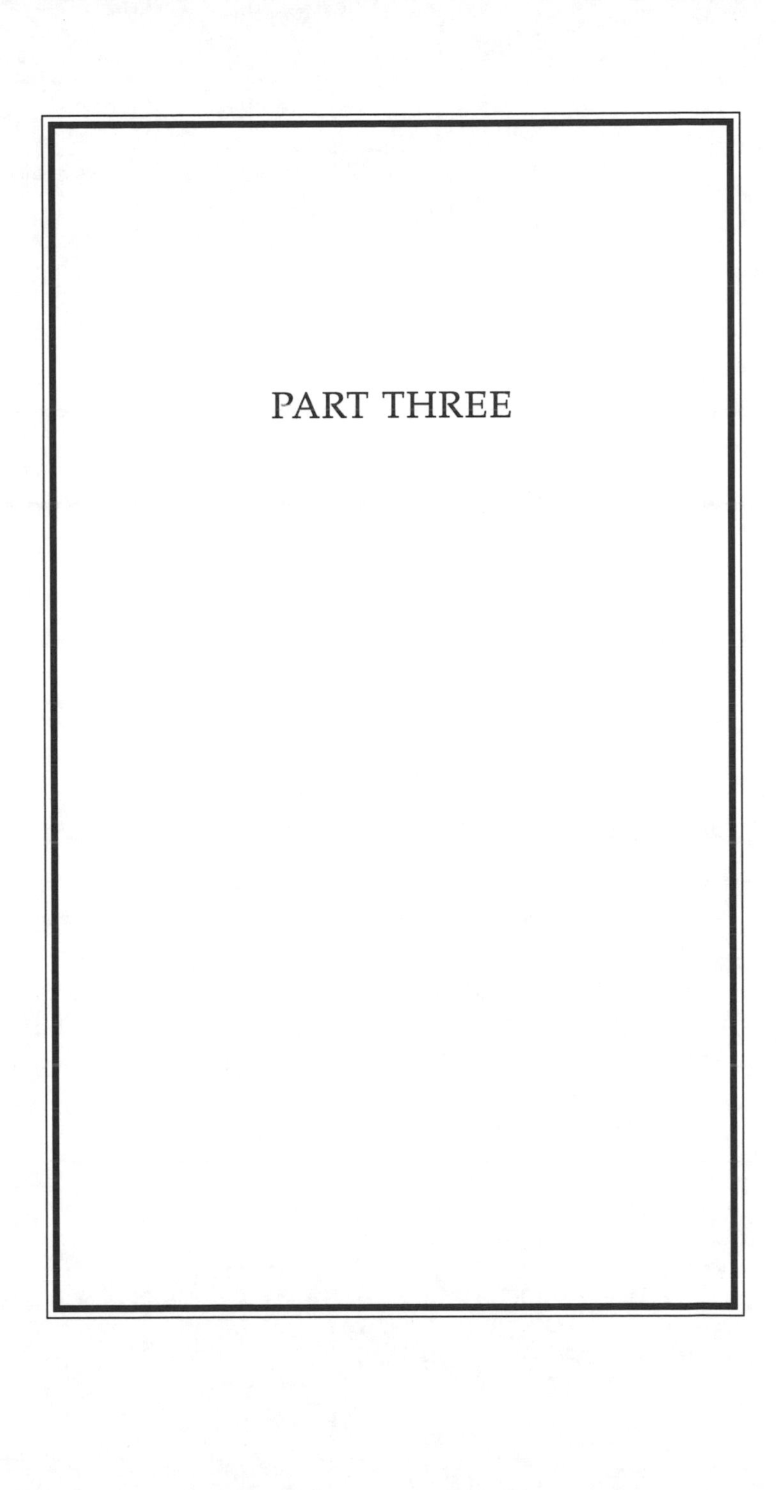

PART THREE

When the timer rang she knew she would not be able to put on a show. She would give anything to get that jeep going but there was no way without a push. So she put away her baton and got on her bicycle and rode down the lane, not straight toward cemetery road and town but the other way that eventually brought you back to town though it took much longer. This way you rode to the far end of their lane, then you turned onto a high road which wound along the edge of the foothills, with the whole green valley spread below.

This was how they came for Sunday rides, in the winter when Dad wasn't so busy. They would drive along slowly, listening to Jack Benny, Dad in his good hat and smoking a cigar, driving all the roads in the valley, looking to see if anything had happened anywhere, noticing a fixed fence or a new colt or a garden dug up early.

The first part of the road was steep going on a bike, and she stood on the pedals, until she got up the little rise past Stevens' and then could peddle easily along the smooth oiled road.

She rode cautiously, ready to put on a spurt of speed, then lift both feet to the handlebars if Stevens' mean dogs ran out snapping. But no dogs appeared and once she was past there she could coast, listening to the bugs buzzing in the sagebrush on the foothills, buzzing more sleepily now that the sun was low. To the south Sheep Mountain rose up like a big blue ice cube, floating above the hills, cooling everything down from the hot day. As it cooled, a breath seemed to rise from the valley and the sweet smell of new cut hay from below mixed with the lonesome smell of sagebrush from the hills.

The valley from up here looked better than when you were down in it, seeing all the saggy barbed wire fences and nothing but corn on one side and hay on the other. From down there it seemed people just did what they could to get by. From up here there seemed to be a plan, the squared fields all a slightly different shade of green or brown or gold, making a flat quilt which seemed delicate and complicated. But this was not at all how it had looked when Thomas Pratt came. Then it had all been sagebrush and frizzy yellow hill grass, the valley no better than the foothills, just one big Dry Gulch.

The first thing they did when they came from Kentucky was dig the ditch, everybody out digging in a big crew with the women taking up picnic dinner to where the men were working. The ditch brought water down from Strike Creek and all the different farms had their rights to water, the best water rights going to those that had been settled longest. Now all you had to do was go out and put boards in the ditch box when you wanted water, and the water would flood out on your field.

There had only been one summer in Alberta's memory that there was trouble over irrigation water. That was a year when it had barely snowed and Strike Creek was low, so low you could cross on rocks and boulders, even in the high water of spring, without getting your feet wet. Then water was low the next summer and everyone was nervous. And sure enough, somebody started stealing water, sneaking out at night and turning water off other people's fields and putting it onto his own. He would let it run all night until early in the morning when he would sneak out and put it back the way it had been. So the men whose water was stolen had gone to the ditch walker, Mike Danner. Do your job, they told him, or let somebody else do it. And some of them loaded their deer rifles. That night Mike Danner hid out and caught the man doing it, one of the Stevens boys people said, and they fought with shovels by the ditch. What happened then had faded away. But Alberta could see them there in the wet night, their irrigating boots squelching in the ditch-bank mud, their shovel blades upraised and shining in the darkness.

If there was a shovel fight this summer she and Martha Lee would hide and watch. But there was plenty of water and not much chance.

Now with everything set in the valley, the ditches all dug, the fields all fenced off, it looked like the people here would think of something else to do besides grow corn and hay and feed cattle. It seemed like they would get tired of doing the same thing over and over.

Why for example hadn't they tried to build a real town here with a dime store and an airport and side-walks along both sides of the road?

Had it ever crossed their minds to have a better town, or had they all said to each other a hundred years ago when they were coming from Kentucky, "Let's not fool with a town. One store is enough and maybe a couple of pool halls and some churches."

Or had they wanted a town? Because once there had been a bank in Adair and a hotel where people stopped when they came through on the stage.

There had been a movie house one time, and once they had tried to build a community center. They had dug a big hole for it right on Main Street. Next they had put up a foundation of cinder blocks as high as your knee. But they never finished it and for a long time just the cinder blocks sat there. Finally somebody built another pool hall on top of them so that now there were two pool halls, though neither one ever had more than a couple of cars or pickups in front.

Maybe they had wanted a better town but weren't able to get it so finally everybody gave up and just drove to Bonner when they wanted something.

Now she came around the crest of the hill and started down the long grade that would let her coast all the way to the grade school and past the "Entering Adair, pop. 198" sign. She sat back and flew, the warm wind filling her mouth, which she kept open, though with her teeth closed, otherwise gnats would blow right down your throat.

She flew, her head empty of all but wind, until she began to slow down at Huff's milk barn, and then had to start peddling at the corner of the grade school.

She noticed, as she could never help doing, the sign on a fence across the road from the school saying, "Sale Everthing Gos." The sign embarrassed her. She thought of people driving by, seeing the school, then the sign and saying, "That must be some school." She would like to take it down. Nothing was on sale anyway. Somebody had put it up long ago and then forgotten it. But the sign was a board nailed on a post, too hard to get down, and she peddled on toward town down into the hotter thicker air on the valley floor. In a sudden wave the town smell of burnt wood from the hotel fire replaced the sagebrush and hay smell of the foot-hill road.

She rode fast going by where the old hotel had been. After the fire, some people named Robins had pulled a little tin trailer house up beside the mess of charred wood. They had parked right on the scorched ground and were living there, somehow cramming all nine or ten of themselves inside. She rode past them fast, partly because she despised the nasty burnt smell, partly because she was a little afraid of the Robinses. Nobody knew where they came from or why they had picked the valley. Did they say, whenever they heard about a fire, I bet that lot will be vacant. Let's move there.

Nobody had seen any Mr. Robins, but you could see Mrs. Robins almost any day, walking from her trailer to the store and back. She was low to the ground with long black hair and a rolling walk on little turned-out feet. The turned-out feet made people talking in the store guess she was an Indian, maybe off some reservation in Central Oregon and people said, Are they letting them all go? Delores Buckner who worked at the store told what Mrs. Robins bought, nothing too unusual except they seemed to get a lot of little canned weenies.

And nobody had really had much to do with them except one summer night when there was a potluck supper in the Methodist church yard. Then the Robinses had all walked over from their trailer, seven or so of them with only a little jar of pickles to put on the table, and their plates and forks. Later some people said, Well if they mean to come to church. But everybody was relieved when they didn't.

At dinner one day DeWayne said the Robinses were parked by the old hotel because they didn't want to pay the fifteen dollars a month for the trailer court and that they were just mooching on town property.

"Somebody should do something," DeWayne said. "They ought to run them off like they did with the Chinese."

And he told how in the old days a Chinese family moved into the valley and a big crowd of men went up to see them. Leave the valley by sundown, they told the Chinese and the Chinese did.

But that was probably just something somebody made up. There probably had never been any Chinese anywhere near here.

Anyway nobody told the Robinses to leave and so they kept living there, running water through a hose from a spigot of the old hotel's that still worked, though people you heard talking in the store said, Who's paying for that water? DeWayne said, These trailer houses make it so anybody can plunk down anywhere. Grandma said, There were never people like that in the valley before.

To Alberta it seemed interesting to have the Robinses, just like it would have been interesting to have some Chinese, she didn't see what they could hurt. And as she rode by their trailer, so hot and ugly on the burnt ground, she wished she could sit and watch them go in and out and try to count how many they got inside at once.

But you had to be careful around them. Because once she had been playing in the school yard with Ricky Robins and had kicked him in the shins. He was a big boy, the most Indian-looking of all the Robinses, and so shy he turned his face to the wall when he walked in the school hall. She kicked him, really, to be nice, since the girls always kicked the boys and the boys liked it. It showed you were just a girl and couldn't hurt them so you could kick all you wanted. But after she kicked Ricky Robins he had turned around and slugged her in the stomach so hard she couldn't breathe.

So she didn't dare fool with the Robinses at all and rode past with barely a look, then past the feedmill where the sidewalk started. Then on by the store, the best building in Adair, the only really townish one. It was a high green box with white trim, standing tall among the crouching brown buildings with their ordinary peaked roofs.

Recently the Buckners had gotten a television set and set it up in the store window, so you could stand outside and look at it or you could sit on the flour sacks inside and look at it. But it didn't get a good picture since reception couldn't get over the mountains from the television station in Boise. People talking in the store said the television people were building a tower in Boise that would send reception this far. Other people said they doubted reception would ever get to the valley. Grandma said, Of course it won't, and gave a deep snort every time television was mentioned. When she had to walk by the set at the store she would look at it with a little smile.

Now Alberta rode slowly past the store, seeing herself, coasting and staring, in the darkened windows, seeing herself briefly on the television screen. She was certain they would get reception one day.

She rode on, past the old bank, a small building of stone with 1912 carved in one of the blocks. Its windows had been boarded up since she could remember and there were so many weeds and brambles growing on it you would need a chainsaw to get to the door.

Beside the bank was the phone booth made of cinder blocks. You could use it if you didn't want anybody to listen in on the party line and Alberta always looked to see if Mama was in it, making secret arrangements.

Next came the Swish Inn and attached to the Swish Inn was a poolhall with its windows blacked out. You couldn't see in even when the door opened, it was so dark inside, but if you went close you could smell the liquor they'd gotten drunk and spilled on the floor.

The sidewalk stopped at the poolhall, which marked the end of town like the feedmill marked the beginning. The other poolhall, put up where the community center was supposed to have gone, was a ways down, really past town. It also had a restaurant attached to it, and when it first opened they went up to sit at a little table against the cinderblock wall with a red plastic table cloth. They had hamburgers and milk shakes and Alberta played "I Got Spurs that Jingle Jangle Jingle" on the juke box. But after they had seen it once they had never thought of going again and it didn't seem anybody else went either.

That was it for main street. There were two other streets, back streets of houses and Baird's garage and the two churches.

Maybe she would draw a map and put every single building in Adair on it. Then she might get written up in the paper as she had done a year ago for finding out the valley's population. She had done that by taking the phone book and putting a figure beside every phone number for how many people lived there, then adding in people she knew didn't have a phone and finally coming up with the population of the valley, four hundred and twelve people. It was the first time anybody had seen a figure for the valley. The government just added the valley into the county.

"Send it in to Edna," several people had said, so Alberta did, and got her first item in the paper even though Edna had written it up, "There are 412 folk residing in our valley, according to a survey taken by little Alberta Whiting, age 10."

This would get a better write-up, and if she hurried she might get it while Martha Lee was here. First she would ride through the town, and map that. Then, if she could just get the jeep going, she could do the whole valley, driving over every road, drawing a map as she went. She would put in houses, barns, silos, chicken houses, everything.

Or, why not build a model of the valley, making the landscape out of plaster of Paris. It would show the road she'd just ridden on, high above the fields, then the steep road down into town. The road would rise again as it went on up to Sparta and possibly you could even see the ghost town and the creek and Uncle Edmund's shack. Grandma could knit the fields, in green, gold and brown, then there would be a tiny Johnny Rexley with a gun out hunting the ducks. Looming at one end of the valley would be a big Sheep Mountain of cardboard, painted light blue. When it was done you would be able to see everything as if looking down from an airplane.

She rode fast down Adair's second street, a street she now named United Christian Street, since all the streets and roads would have names printed down the middle.

She would name the streets and roads since nobody else had bothered to do it. And forever more when people used a name it would be the name she had given, whether they knew it or not.

She rode to the end of the street, then turned and started back slowly so as to look at everything in order. Next to the United Christian Church was the United

Christian parsonage and next to the parsonage was a white building called City Hall, a little white house with the porch falling off and the door always padlocked shut. She didn't know why it was called City Hall.

Next to the City Hall was an unpainted house where Old Man Decker had always lived, sitting on his porch and yelling when you went by that he didn't want a subscription. Next to him was an ugly house covered with red paper made to look like bricks. It was the ugliest house in town, usually rented to a teacher.

She hated that ugly house and was tempted to leave it off. But no, she would put in everything, like it or not. She would put in the trailers too, made out of little matchboxes covered with tin foil. She would put in the Robins trailer and burnt matchsticks to show the remains of the hotel. She would put in Old Man Rexley's truck on its way to the liquor store.

Next to the teachers' house was the gray sagging old shack that used to be the livery stable and where Uncle Edmund said the old sheepherder's bones were buried and she stopped her bike and went around behind the livery stable to see if there was any bump or other sign of a grave.

What if she went and got a shovel right now and tried to dig up those bones before Martha Lee got here? Then she would get written up in the paper for sure and maybe have to go to Bonner and testify at a trial.

She lay down her bike and found a stick to dig with in the dirt behind the old stable. Since it had been deserted so long, nobody had been driving up to it and the ground was pretty soft. But you might have to dig twenty or thirty holes before you found the bones. So she got back on her bike and finished riding down Christian Street, rode up the next street that would be called Methodist Street, then turned to look for the big green store, which would be the centerpiece of town, the one good building, rising above the low brown roofs. But from here she couldn't see the store which seemed funny. She turned and rode back toward Main Street but the big green store seemed to have disappeared.

She rode back to Main Street, turned onto it and went past the Swish Inn, where a pickup pulling a horse trailer was now parked, past the little old bank, and there, of course, was the store, big and green as ever. She saw herself frowning in the darkened plate glass windows.

She got off the bike and pushed it through the alley beside the store where the mailman parked in the morning to pick up his mail sack. She went on, through the weeds and broken bottles around to the back of the store. But the back of the store was not high and green, only a low brown roof like every other roof. Its green front was a fake, a wall of boards that stood up in front of the real roof. They hadn't even bothered to paint it green in back. But they had still fooled her all this time.

She got back on her bike and rode out to Main Street. Why couldn't they have gone ahead and built one good store? But it seemed like people here would rather pretend than anything.

Her store would still be a good one, a nice square box, covered with green paper, front and back.

But then, if you were going to start changing things, why not really change them? Why not put in two stores and a movie? Why not put in an airport with an airplane hanging from the ceiling that was supposed to be coming in for a landing? Why not give themselves a fine big house with a wide bay window?

Would it be better to make a real place that had hardly anything, or a pretend place that had whatever you wanted?

She would put in the trailer court anyway, and the vein of gold shooting through the hillside up by Sparta.

She turned and rode back up Main Street, then turned

onto a little lane that led to what used to be Booker's cow pasture and still was at the back. The front of the pasture, though, had been turned into a trailer court.

The trailers were parked at a slant from the road that went through the court and all of them had some kind of lean-to built on. The lean-tos were covered with different things, black tar paper or boards, even screen windows. Alberta had ridden through the trailer court once before but very fast. Now, going slower, she saw that the trailers and lean-tos were all different. Some were big messes, with junk spilling out the door onto the ground, some were very neat and one, the one with the screened lean-to, even had a little white fence around it. It was hard to see how they had the heart to put up a white fence when they would just have to take it down again when they moved.

In front of one trailer a fat woman was watering her skimpy patch of grass with a hose. She had a cigarette dangling in her mouth and bare fat legs and a bathrobe barely closed over her big bosom. Alberta rode fast since this was the kind of thing you feared when you went someplace like a trailer court.

All the doors and windows of the trailers seemed to be open and as she rode between them on the dirt road Alberta could hear the different sounds coming from each one. From one, where she was pretty sure Hank's girlfriend Shirley lived, she heard the sound of somebody arguing. From two trailers came the radio news, and from the trailer at the end of the row, which she was now passing, came the sound of "Wake Up Little Susie." She knew for certain who lived there, Darla Knight, one of the girls from baton. She also knew it was Darla's high school sister, Jeanette, playing records. They had only been here a few months, and didn't have a mother, only a father who drove a truck and was always gone.

She rode past Darla's trailer and circled the wash house at the end of the road where sheets were hanging on clotheslines. Beyond the wash house was a barbed wire fence and beyond it the cow pasture started up again.

Darla was a year older than Alberta and wore smeary red lipstick, but she was always nice and jokey so Alberta rode slowly past, then to the end of the trailer court, then back again and when she didn't see Darla she got off her bike anyway and propped it against the lean-to. She knocked at the lean-to door feeling shy, but on the other hand reckless, as if in a trailer court you could do whatever came to mind.

When Darla looked up from where she was lying on the couch and saw her outside the door she only said, "Oh hi," as if Alberta came every day. Darla had short spikey hair and was chubby and as she lay on the couch barefoot she picked between her toes. Still Alberta liked her and the easy, casual way she had as if she didn't care so much about every little thing. Alberta went in and sat on the arm of the couch with her legs spraddled out. It was the only place to sit in the trailer since Darla's high school sister Jeanette was using the kitchen table to iron and blocking all the table chairs.

"Put that on again," Jeanette said and Darla got up and went back to where the record player had been coming from. Jeanette didn't say anything to Alberta, but since she seemed to look at her in the same crabby high schoolish way she looked at Darla, Alberta didn't mind and even liked it. It was as if, in a tiny way, she was one of the sisters too, sitting around the trailer listening to records. It wasn't anything like being around a bunch of Lacey cousins who, no matter what they did, did it in some loud Lacey way that you just couldn't match even if you tried.

"Wake Up Little Susie" started and Alberta hoped Jeanette would dance around, but she didn't seem to notice the record and kept ironing with a frown on her face. She was blonde, her hair done up in rows of perfect round pin curls. She wasn't really cute, yet there was some look about her all the high school girls tried to copy, something everybody liked and Alberta was glad to sit and study what it was.

There was no telling where their father was or what had happened to their mother. It was a shame they didn't have a mother, but it was nice to have the whole place to yourself.

She looked around the trailer to see if there were pictures of their mother. If the pictures were real old that would mean she was dead. But there were no pictures or knickknacks of any kind.

But she loved the trailer, the little table where Jeanette was ironing and the cute little built-in kitchen with a little refrigerator and a little sink. She wished she could go back and see the tiny bathroom and their beds, but she didn't want to act like she'd never been in a trailer so she didn't ask to look. Pretty soon she would say she had to go to the toilet.

You could imagine just Darla and Jeanette living here alone, with no parents or grandparents or any particular place they were from. Alberta wondered if that was what made Darla seem so free and loose. Probably not, because Jeanette was not free and loose, she was always serious. Alberta knew from seeing Jeanette walking with the high school girls that she always had a frown on her face and that she wore the exact same thing every day: white flats, full skirt with at least two can-cans underneath, sleeveless white blouse with a little collar and a silk scarf around the neck, either black or yellow. Other high school girls had started trying to dress this way, but none of them got it right. Either the blouse wasn't right, with ruffles or long sleeves, or their skirts weren't full enough to float on top of the can-cans the way Jeanette's did. Instead of floating, their skirts bulged too tight over the can-cans, making the girls look like they'd been stuffed in a sack. Or they would put on a scarf with cats or something on it.

Before they came here, Jeanette and Darla had lived

in Hagerman, Idaho which they both wanted to go back to especially Jeanette. When they were there, Darla had told Alberta, Jeanette had a job in the dime store and the cutest boy for her boy friend and if they had stayed Jeanette could have been cheerleader. This was at a big school with 200 kids, four times as big as the valley school where there were only forty kids. In Hagerman they played eleven man football instead of eight and had six cheerleaders instead of three.

"Jeanette could be cheerleader here," Alberta had said, because she had watched the cheerleaders carefully at the high school football games. There was one cute cheerleader, a town girl whose father ran one of the gas stations. But she was practically the only cute girl in high school. The other two cheerleaders were Laceys, heavy-legged and lumbering in their yellow pleated skirts and sometimes when they did a cheer and jumped up in the air, the men standing on the sidelines would stagger and pretend the earth shook when they came back down.

But Darla said Jeanette wasn't going to even try out because she wasn't going to stay here long enough to be cheerleader.

They put on "Wake Up Little Susie" several more times and Alberta felt happy sitting there with them, picking at the scab on her knee and pretending to be as casual as Darla, and at the same time watching Jeanette iron. It was exciting to know Jeanette was so determined to go someplace.

She wished Jeanette would say something and especially that she would talk about her plans for getting back to Hagerman or whatever she planned to do. She wanted Jeanette to talk so much that when the music stopped and Darla went back to put it on again, Alberta took a chance and said, "Do you know Hank Hopper? He works for us. They all say Shirley Duncan is trying to get him to get married but he won't. They kid all the time. They kid him about his car too."

Jeanette looked up from the ironing but didn't say anything and Alberta flushed hot. After ages Jeanette said, "I wouldn't marry him if my life depended on it."

"Me either," Alberta said quickly.

"He asked me out and I said, 'Like fun,'" Jeanette said.

Alberta couldn't think of a reply, confused to have turned against Hank. Still she wanted Jeanette to keep talking.

"Who would you like to go out with here?" Alberta asked, knowing it was a risk. "Anybody?"

Jeanette seemed interested in the question and to be thinking. Alberta dared to stretch out on the couch since Darla hadn't come back yet.

"There's this guy over in Six Mile," Jeanette said finally, speaking of the next valley.

"What's he like?" Alberta asked, feeling that she was getting the hang of it and could carry on for a long time. She hoped Darla wouldn't come back right away.

Jeanette shrugged said, "His mother lets you hang around the house. I like somebody you can go to their house."

"Why?"

"I like houses. I like all the furniture and everything."

It didn't sound like much fun just going to a house and Alberta said, "You know what? You ought to be an airline stewardess."

It seemed this would be the perfect thing for Jeanette with her carefully controlled outfit and hairdo.

"Yeah," Jeanette said. "Maybe."

Alberta almost loved Jeanette for planning to go someplace like she herself secretly planned to. She wanted to talk about where they might go, feeling that Jeanette with her trailer court life and no farm to inherit would know better what you could do. But Jeanette was a grouchy high school girl, and Alberta had to be careful, so she tried to say more things she thought Jeanette would like.

"I really bet you could be a stewardess easy," Alberta said.

"How do you get to be one?" Jeanette asked.

"Well," Alberta said. "I had a book about it. There's a school where they teach you. You have to be real pretty and not over five-foot-eight. You could get in I bet."

Jeanette ironed and Alberta watched to see if she would soften up at this compliment. Finally Jeanette said, "A girlfriend of mine in Hagerman went to beauty school."

"Well," Alberta said. "I wouldn't want to smell permanents all day." Then, since Jeanette didn't seem interested in the stewardess idea, she told about Uncle Edmund's daughter Joanne who had gone to Boise and gotten a job at the Royal Hotel, and about her cute little booth in the lobby where she once sold a pack of gum to Bob Hope.

"She doesn't go to work until three so she sleeps late and has breakfast at noon," Alberta said. "Then she is there until midnight all dressed up. You should see these sea shell earrings she has."

"How did she get the job?" Jeanette asked.

Alberta didn't know but said, "She just got real dressed up and went in and they gave it to her."

"Is she real pretty?"

"Yes," Alberta said. "And while she was there she met a French guy and she brought him out to visit. He wore a suit and tan socks with clocks on them and these pants there were a kind of oatmeal-colored material. He would lounge back on the davenport and let all his change fall in the cushions and not even pick it up. Boy. And he took a bath every afternoon. He used up so much hot water we had to wait until ten o'clock to wash the supper dishes."

"Did she marry him?"

Alberta said, "Boy was he cute too. He had wavy black hair that if you touched it was just stiff."

"How come you touched it?" Darla asked, who had just come out to get a funny book from by the couch.

"I just bumped it by accident when I went behind his chair," Alberta said. "And it didn't budge."

Darla got the funny book and went back in to flop on the bed again. Jeanette said, "He just came in the hotel and asked her for a date?"

"Yes," Alberta said, making up this part. "She was standing there in her little booth and he came up and asked in his French accent if they had cigars."

"Then what?"

"Well she said yes they did and he said he wanted a whole box. Then he told Joanne she had pretty hair and asked her if she dyed it."

"Did she?"

"Yeah, real blonde. Also she wore one of those pointed brassieres. It was so pointed sometimes the point would get pushed in and stay that way and she wouldn't even notice."

"She should stuff it with Kleenex," Jeanette said.

"Yeah. She should."

"What did he do after he got the cigars?"

"Well, he asked her if she wanted go the movies to see Jerry Lewis."

"Did they get married?"

Alberta wanted to talk more about their dates. She was going to have them ballroom dancing next, and then swimming at a pool diving off the diving board. But she had to say, "No, he turned out to be married already."

"Yeah," Jeanette said.

"I still want to go to France. Don't you? Have you ever looked at France on the map? You wouldn't believe how close together everything is in France. All the little roads and towns just jammed together and no big lonesome places at all. They're Catholics there though, but I don't think it matters that much. Do you?"

When Jeanette didn't answer she switched and said,

"Or Washington D.C. I would love to go there. I did a whole project about it once. Boy I'd love to see that huge Lincoln sitting in his chair."

"I'm only praying to get back to Hagerman," Jeanette said, "and not get stuck here."

"What about Lapland?" Alberta asked. "I read about houses there where you sleep in big cupboards. You get in bed, then close the door and you're safe inside this cupboard."

"I just want a regular house," Jeanette said. "I don't care what kind of cupboards it has. I might settle for a doublewide trailer to start off. Some of those doublewides you can hardly tell from a house."

"Do you expect you'll get dishes and crystal when you get married?" Alberta asked.

"Sure you have to have dishes," Jeanette said.

Alberta felt the conversation was about to end. So she went ahead and told about her cousin coming from Japan, landing tonight at the Bonner airport. Then, because Jeanette didn't reply and because she knew Jeanette was seventeen she said, "Just think. When Thomas Pratt my great-grandfather was seventeen he came out West from Kentucky all by himself. He practically discovered this whole valley when he was just your age."

In fact he had been eighteen but it was close enough and it was interesting to look at Jeanette and see what a person that age could do. Though it didn't really seem like Jeanette was going to do much. Alberta enjoyed trying to talk to Jeanette and admired her as a high school girl who everybody tried to copy, but she wished Jeanette had better plans.

Jeanette didn't comment on Thomas Pratt and it seemed like time to go. Alberta went back to where Darla was reading a funny book on the double bed that filled up the whole back of the trailer. To get there she had to pass two bunkbeds on the right, with cute little windows where Darla and Jeanette slept. She would keep trying to be friends with them so maybe they would invite her to spend the night and sleep in one of the bunkbeds sometime. She used the bathroom, no bigger than a closet and with only a blue plastic tub hanging on the wall which they must have used as a bathtub somehow. She said goodbye in the casual way Darla and Jeanette did things and went back out in the trailer court which now was baking hot and smelled of frying. It was so hot the strong food smells were sickening and she rode fast to get out. Still it was good to have stayed so long and gotten Jeanette to carry on such a long conversation.

She rode through town and down cemetery lane, then turned onto their road. As she got closer to their place she saw a cloud of dust rising from the lane which was the men all driving back up from the hay field, first Dad's red pickup, then Hank following in his black car with the coon tail flying. Alberta sped up to meet them at the corner, to see if they were on their way to the pool hall and if they had wild looks on their faces.

But they were already drinking beer, Junior sitting in the back of the pickup with a bottle of beer in his hand and Dad and DeWayne both in the cab with beers. They looked maybe a little wilder than usual or maybe it was only the black hay dirt that made their eyes seem white and staring.

"Put your bike in the back and go swimming with us," Dad said and after hesitating a second she did, feeling that it was a little dangerous but on the other hand it might keep them from getting too drunk if she was there.

Behind the pickup Hank waited in his black car, Shirley cuddled up next to him in the front seat, her fat white face nestling in long whitish hair.

Alberta climbed up in the back of the pickup with Junior, who sat up on the side, looking out over the cab. Alberta sat on the floor as a precaution against drunk driving.

They went down the road, past their two houses which

sat silent and calm under the big tree, so peaceful-looking that you would never guess Mama was in one house, crying because things weren't pretty, and Grandma was in the other, in a rage over burial spots.

They drove on by, tooting the horn and making a kind of parade down to the reservoir. Alberta sat backwards and watched Hank's coon tail flying, trying to make out whether he had his arm around Shirley and was using the green suicide knob to drive.

They drove along the flat valley floor, past the irrigated fields of corn and hay that stood up thick and green in the early evening, giving off a juice-filled smell. Then they began to wind down, down from the level irrigated fields to the part that wasn't irrigated and it was like going into a different poorer country where it was hotter and more tiring with only dusty purple sagebrush holding the dirt onto the hillside. And then down and down some more into the hot river canyon where once the Snake River had twisted thinly through with nobody but Indians to see it. Now Idaho Power had dammed it up to get electricity, also giving them a reservoir to swim in, though the water was greenish from standing still.

At the reservoir they crunched up into the gravel parking lot, past the signs that said Beware of Rattlesnakes and the barrels that said Deposit Fish Waste Here. They parked beside a pickup with a boat trailer on it, probably belonging to somebody from Bonner. Alberta scanned the reservoir for the boat but it must have gone on down the canyon. There were, though, two high-school looking girls in two-piece swimming suits lying stretched out face down on the raft that floated on the edge of the reservoir.

The hay men climbed out and stood staring down to where the girls lay but they had gone quiet and nobody mentioned them. One of the girls raised up and started hunting in her bag and took out a cigarette and put it in her mouth. Then she hunted some more but didn't find anything and finally threw the cigarette back in her bag.

"One of you boys go down and give her a light," DeWayne said and everybody laughed but sounded kind of strange.

Dad and the hay men went behind the pickup to change into their trunks, but Shirley didn't get out of the car or lean out to speak. Alberta went to sit on the pick-up's front fender and kept her eyes carefully forward while the men changed. Below the girls on the raft lay like dolls, their arms thrown over their heads, one in a green two-piece, one in black. Neither had glanced up once to see who might have come.

Now the men came back around the pickup wearing only their swimming trunks with their boots flapping loose and unlaced around their ankles. It was a shock to see them, their necks and muscular arms bright red and covered with black hay dust, their chests brown, then their legs, white and skinny in the sockless boots. Their foreheads were white too where their hats usually went, giving their heads a sickish look.

They seemed to know they were funny-looking and not themselves. They didn't speak to Alberta or Shirley, but all went scrambling down the side of the hill to the water, beer bottles in their hands. They looked so silly on their white stick legs that Alberta turned her eyes away to study the dry hills on the other side of the reservoir, where a line of shadows crept up from the water, as if trying to put out the still-sunny hilltop.

But she looked back when they got down to the water, how they piled up their boots at the edge and stood around for a minute, and then, instead of going onto the raft to jump in as people ordinarily did, they waded quietly into the greenish water. The two girls on the raft didn't raise up or even turn their heads.

In Hank's car Shirley was brushing her long white-blonde hair. She hadn't even looked down to the reservoir and so didn't know the girls were there.

"Aren't you going swimming?" Alberta finally went over and said to her. She had a little turned up nose and dark blue eyes, and was pretty, maybe, if you liked people this puffy. She had on cutoffs and a shirt Alberta recognized as Hank's. On her finger she was wearing Hank's class ring. She had put a huge wad of adhesive tape on the ring to make it fit and then painted over the tape with pink fingernail polish so it looked like it had a gob of bubble gum stuck to it.

"Don't you want to go in?" Alberta asked, leaning her elbows on the car door to look in.

"I'm faint," Shirley said. "I haven't had nothing to eat all day but a bowl of Cheerios for breakfast."

"Why not?" Alberta asked.

"I'm on a diet. Since everybody thinks I'm so fat."

"Oh," Alberta said politely. "They don't either."

"Yes they do."

"There's lots of people fatter than you," Alberta said.

Shirley kept brushing her hair holding it up with her white puffy arms.

"I was just up by your place," Alberta said. "I was at Jeanette and Darla's. We were talking about maybe being airline stewardesses. Jeanette would be a perfect airline stewardess."

Shirley didn't say anything and Alberta had to say, "So would you probably."

Shirley didn't say anything and Alberta said, "Is there anything you want to do? Besides get married?"

"Who said I wanted to get married," Shirley asked.

"Well aren't you engaged?"

"Maybe."

"Look," Alberta said. "Is there anyplace you want to go?"

"Home," Shirley said. "I'm faint from this diet."

"Well," Alberta said. "It will probably be a while before they come back. There are two cute girls down there in two-piece swimming suits." Then she turned and went down to the water.

She sat down at the edge of the reservoir and took off her shoes then waded in in her shorts and shirt, the water soft and warm as a bath, the green scum not very thick today and only sticking to your skin in little specks. Some days it was thick as mustard and smelled bad. Nobody knew what made the difference.

Dad and the hay men were now perched on the raft on the other end from where the girls lay, and she paddled out to them. For a while she practiced a method to avoid drowning she'd read about in the *Reader's Digest*. You floated with your face under water holding your breath. Then when you needed to breathe you gave a tiny kick so you could get your nose out and breathe once. That way you stayed afloat without using much energy and could last for days until somebody came to rescue you.

After practicing that for a while she pulled up on the raft between Hank and Dad. She glanced over at the girls to see if they saw her, here with this bunch of beer-drinking men. They might not know she was one of them's daughter. But the girls lay with their heads turned away, still and brown like they were carved from wood.

The hay men started to horse around, Hank pushing Junior in, then Junior swimming back, snorting and blowing and grabbing both Hank and DeWayne by the legs and trying to pull them in. Then Dad picked up Alberta and threw her in and so they started having fun and the men's skinny legs didn't look so bad now that everybody was wet and dripping and jumping around.

Still the girls didn't turn their heads or act like they knew there were a bunch of people on the raft with them.

As they horsed around on their end of the raft they heard a motor boat engine and in a minute saw it come out of the canyon and head toward the dock. The girls lifted their heads as if it was what they had been waiting for. The hay men all stood and watched the boat come, a fancy black motorboat with a windshield and a steering wheel you drove like a car. In it was a man with a big suntanned belly and a cigarette in his teeth, and he swirled the boat around a couple of times to show off for them before he slowed down and headed toward the raft. Junior and Hank reached out and caught the nose of the boat as it drifted in so it wouldn't bump the raft too hard. Meanwhile the raft danced and rocked from the waves the boat set up, so much that the girls had to finally sit up and one of them said to the man, their father probably, "Can we go?"

The man turned off the engine with a switch but then he kept sitting there smoking his cigarette and telling them all about his boat. It was a brand new boat and he'd just picked it up in Boise and brought it right out to the reservoir for its first try-out. The man had wanted a boat with get-up-and-go, he said, that would do something when he wanted it to. Junior and Hank kept holding the boat's nose so it wouldn't bump into the dock while Dad asked questions about the boat, what kind of engine it was and how fast it could go top speed. The man leaned back in the white leather seats telling all about it and smoking.

"Come on," the man said to Dad. "Get in and I'll show you what she can do."

You could tell he wanted to go but he said, "Junior, don't you want to go for a ride?"

Junior shook his head, probably afraid he'd stutter if he said anything in front of the girls.

"How about you boys?" Dad said to DeWayne and Hank, but DeWayne said, "You go ahead," so Dad climbed in while they kept holding the boat. The man said,

"Better put on a life preserver."

Dad said, "I'll hang on."

Junior and Hank pushed them around so they were pointing out and the man went back to start the engine again, yanking it with a cord. He came back and put it in gear and they drove out to the middle, then started turning in big circles so the boat tilted a little and the passenger side where Dad was sitting rose a little ways out of the water. They could see how he held onto the side of the boat and how the big bellied man kept talking and waving one hand, a cigarette still in his teeth. In a minute the waves got to the raft and made it rock so the girls who had lay down again sat back up.

In a minute the boat stopped its turns and sat rocking out in the middle. The man got up and they traded so Dad was in the driver's seat.

They could see the man pointing his finger here and there while Dad nodded his head. Then they seemed to be set and Dad took hold of the wheel. He looked over at them on the raft and waved and while he was still looking and waving the boat shot off, like it had gone without his knowing, so that all the hay men and even the girls laughed. The boat shot down the reservoir and kept going like he didn't know how to stop it or turn it around, and they could see the man leaning toward Dad and pointing down at the controls.

Finally he got it turned and headed back toward them and shot past the other way and again the man leaned over him pointing. Then he got it turned and came back to the middle where he started making big circles.

"Now he's got the hang of it," Hank said.

He kept making circles but the circles got smaller and smaller, the boat tipping more and more, the passenger side starting to rise up high out of the water. The circles kept on getting smaller and the engine went into a high scream as the boat now seemed to stand up on its side, spinning like something under the reservoir had hooked onto it and was trying to pull it straight to the bottom. Dad's elbow was in the water and the big-bellied man hooked one arm around the high side of the boat and reached in back with the other for a life preserver that he hung around his neck. They could see that his mouth was moving and that his cigarette was gone.

Behind them on the raft the girls stood up and one of them said, "He'll flip it," but nobody turned around to answer.

They stood without speaking, Alberta and the haymen lined up on the edge of the raft, their ankles washed with the waves from the boat. Still the boat spun, nearly on its side, looking as if it had to tip over.

"He's trying to get killed, the crazy fool," one of the girls said.

"Shut up," Hank said.

Surely he wouldn't let himself get killed with her watching.

So she didn't take her eyes off until it seemed maybe the circles were getting bigger, then it was certain they were, and finally when the boat wasn't tipping at all any more she jumped off the dock in a belly flop, making a big smack.

"That's a nice boat," Dad said when they came back in. "Thanks for the ride." He turned off the engine and it was terribly quiet.

"You bet," the big-bellied man said stiffly, then snapped at the girls, asking why they hadn't backed the boat trailer down to the edge of the water already if they were so anxious to go.

So the girls packed up their things and left, struggling up the hillside in their rubber sandals. The man started the engine again and drove it off to where the road came down to the water so people could load their boats.

The hay men all jumped in and Dad sat on the dock, dangling his legs in the water. Soon everybody was sitting on the dock, chilly in the shade that now covered the whole canyon and in a while they gathered up their beer bottles and boots and climbed back up to the parking lot where Shirley still sat brushing her hair.

The hay men got in with Hank to open more beer and sit drinking a while, leaving Alberta and Dad to go home in the pickup.

"Is a boat a lot like a plane to drive?" Alberta asked as they crunched out of the parking lot. "Or fly."

"Oh," Dad said. "There's not much to a boat."

"Were you ever in one before?"

"Oh sure. I knew a fella in Alabama who had one. We used to squirrel it around all the time."

It was a relief to know he hadn't been as crazy as he seemed.

She saw him out on a pink Alabama lake, young and sharp faced, one eyebrow cocked as he spun a motor boat round and round until it seemed to rise in the air.

"It's too bad you couldn't have stayed in Alabama," she said.

"It was too hot there," he said.

"Well, it's too bad you couldn't keep flying a plane."

"I don't know that peace-time flying is much fun anyway," he said. "I could have gotten a job flying an airliner."

"What?"

"After the war the recruiters from the airline companies came to see us. They needed pilots."

"You could have gotten a job flying an airliner?"

He nodded, leaning a little against the door of the cab and driving slow as he did sometimes in the evening. She looked at him to see if he was kidding, but he didn't have the slight questioning look in his eye he had when it was a joke.

"Then why didn't you?" she finally asked.

"Well I had flown transport planes a little bit and after a while it got just like driving a bus, back and forth, back and forth."

"But here you just drive a tractor around and around."

"But it's my place."

"It's Grandma's place."

"Well," he said. "I'll inherit it."

They were up now to the valley floor and he kept driving slow, smelling the hay fields and hearing the evening birds squawking. The foothills that ringed the valley were deep violet though the sky was still a pale blue.

"Isn't this a nice time of day," Dad said like he always did in the evening.

But how could he have given up a job flying an airliner?

"Somebody had to take over the place," he said.

"Boy," she said. "I wouldn't have done that. Think of the places you could have gone. France, maybe."

She watched him but he only drove thoughtfully on.

They didn't talk any more until they got home where the lights were already on in the house and you could hear the water gurgling in the ditch, as you always started to hear in the evening. She got her bike down from the pickup and parked it behind the cellar. While she was putting it away she heard Grandma's screen door slam and then her clip-clipping steps along the cement walkway. In a few seconds she heard the whoosh-bang which was Mama closing the kitchen window Grandma was just about to walk by. In a bit she heard the creak of the cellar door and then the click of the cellar light Grandma had turned on. In a second the cellar door creaked again, and Grandma clip-clipped back and you could hear her slow down as she passed their lighted kitchen window. Alberta stood longer in the dark shadows behind the cellar and waited for the next sound, Dad's rubber irrigating boots on the back step, the slam of their back screen door and then the sound of him pulling up a chair on the back porch and the soft plop of his two boots dropping.

They couldn't make a sound she didn't know.

When she went into the house everything was put

away and perfect, the yellow roses glowing like lamps. Mama had on a white dress with yellow piping, taken from the Alabama box and her plump tanned skin shone.

So it seemed that everything anybody could do had been done, and Alberta sat down to the plate of supper, a hamburger and tomato soup, since Mama and Dad were going to have supper at the airport. Alberta could hardly stand not getting to go, and it was only her plan to pretend to be sleeping when Martha Lee came and to spy on her that let her bear it.

"Just dress normally tomorrow," Mama said, "in shorts and a shirt but don't go barefoot."

Alberta felt let down that she was not going to get dressed up, but on the other hand what would you do all day in a dress and good shoes and it would look funny to at some point say, All right, now I'm putting my real clothes back on. Whereas Mama could leave her nice dress on all day.

She ate her soup at the table. Dad came out of the bedroom barefoot but otherwise dressed up in his tan stock pants and a pearl-button shirt, his blond hair combed into waves. He sat down on the davenport and put on his socks and shiny dress boots and you could smell that he had put on Mennons. All dressed, he stood up with a snap and catching her looking at him, winked, with the cocky look of the pilot pictures.

But did he think she forgot how he spent his days, going around and around in a black cloud of hay dust just to chop Grandma's hay?

Before Alberta finished her supper they were ready to go and she watched them out the door, watched how they nearly buzzed with the excitement of being so dressed up and handsome.

Then there was nothing to do but take her plate with its half-eaten hamburger though the dark to Grandma's.

They sat at Grandma's kitchen table, looking out over the cornfield and the last pink line of light behind the

Indians marching. Alberta finished the hamburger, then poured them both iced tea from the pitcher in the refrigerator.

They sat watching the last light, and it seemed that they were waiting, not just for the cousin but for something that was meant to come or something that was meant to happen. It seemed that Grandma especially was waiting, always waiting, because certainly you could not sit at a table, night after night, watching the pink light and hearing the ditch go by without expecting or anyway hoping something would eventually come.

Could it be Jesus she sat here and waited for?

Alberta didn't want Jesus to come yet. She didn't want everything to melt away before she got a start.

Maybe it was Thomas Pratt Grandma waited for, so he could come back and take charge and they would have the biggest spread in the valley and be rich again. He could build another house with a wide bay window.

Alberta was waiting for Martha Lee, but that was only the first step.

"I wish they'd hurry up and get here," she said.

"I hope none of them are sick," Grandma said. "There are lots of foreign diseases we haven't got any resistance to."

"I hope they are sick," Alberta said. "I want to start building my resistance."

"You don't want any such thing," Grandma said.

"Yes I do. I'm going to fly everywhere." She saw herself rich with two white suitcases, sitting in an airplane with her seat belt fastened, chewing gum so her ears wouldn't hurt and looking down to see the earth turn below.

"Fiddlesticks," Grandma said.

"Were you rich when you were my age?" Alberta asked.

"We never thought about it that way," Grandma said, "or ever let on like we were, but we always had what we needed."

"Is that all? You had what you needed?"

"I will say," Grandma said, "that Papa had the best smoke house in the country and the best smoked hams which he did himself. And down in the barn there were barrels full of every kind of thing, apples and pears from the orchard out here, pickles and apple butter he made up himself. Oh and apricots he would dry and every kind of thing."

"Did you order lots of clothes from the catalog?"

"Why we had everything we needed. People didn't think they had to have everything store-bought in those days."

"Did you have store-bought cupcakes?" Alberta asked but Grandma didn't reply.

"Well," Alberta said, going back to the conversation. "I don't think that's rich, just having what you needed." It wasn't like you absolutely needed sweaters from the catalog or oranges in your lunch or a maid to fix a different thing every morning for breakfast.

"Of course we held a good deal of property," Grandma said.

"What was your favorite thing you had?" Alberta asked. "When you were my age."

"Well," Grandma said, looking upward to think. "I got a sweet little sewing box one Christmas when I was eleven, all satin inside with compartments for your different notions."

"In your stocking or under the tree?" Alberta asked, to see if the sewing box had been considered a big present or a small one.

"It wasn't the same as you do now," Grandma said. "People didn't put up their own Christmas tree. They would open up the Oddfellows Hall and put two big trees on each side of the stage and then there would be a community program and singing and all the children got candy and popcorn. If you wanted to give a gift to a child you could have it put on the Christmas tree for Santa to give out."

"That's how you got your presents?"

"Some people brought their presents up to give out in public," Grandma said. "We didn't do it that way, because Papa thought it was show-offy."

"So you didn't get any?"

"We got ours at home," Grandma said.

"You never got any from Santa?"

"Some children didn't get gifts from Santa," Grandma said.

"It looks like they could have just taken up one little present," Alberta said.

"Papa didn't like show," Grandma said.

"Yeah but something little."

"Well," Grandma said. "I always thought it was a little bad some children didn't get anything from Santa. But one year, my name was called by Santa and I went up and there was the sweetest little sewing box."

"From your parents?"

"No, from my cousin Floyd."

"The one whose whiskey you poured in the ditch?"

"Yes," Grandma said. "It wasn't any good for Floyd to be getting that old stuff."

"Did he get drunk when he had it?" Alberta asked, remembering Floyd only as a little old man with a sad grin and pants that drooped over his shoes who was now dead.

"I don't know," Grandma said. "I would never have been near it if he had. Girls didn't go hither and yon then. We were never allowed to go to the barn or out in the field when there were men."

"Why not?"

"Papa didn't think it was ladylike. And things were more strict then. For instance, if we ever saw a bull or a boar we wouldn't call it by that name."

"What did you call it?"

"We would say 'critter.' Instead of saying, 'The black bull is in the yard,' we would say, 'The black critter is in the yard.'"

"That sounds silly," Alberta said, who went down to where they worked cattle in front of the barn and saw branding and doctoring and everything. She even helped run with the branding irons, back and forth from the fire to the chute were the steers were caught. She stood there stonily while their hair and skin scorched and they bawled and bellowed. But it only seemed to hurt them for a second, then they were back to normal. The only time she was sent to the house was if something was going to be born.

"Maybe I would almost agree with you about that particular thing," Grandma said. "But in those days there were lots of old ruffians around. The sheepherders would come down from the hills and get drunk and you never knew what would go on."

"What did saying 'The black bull's in the yard' have to do with ruffians?"

"Well," Grandma said. "You had to be extra careful."

"So maybe they did kill that Joe Meek and bury him beside the stable like Uncle Edmund said. If it was so rough."

Grandma sniffed and didn't reply for a while then said, "Papa fired Floyd the next summer and I was so sad when he left."

"Why did he fire him?"

"One day at breakfast Papa said to Floyd, 'You were gone the last eighteen nights out of twenty and you can't do your work that way.'"

"Where had he been?"

"Oh out visiting. He just liked to see people and visit. But I'm sure Papa was right, he wore himself out and then was tired out working."

"Didn't your papa warn him once?"

"No, that wasn't his way."

They sat for a while in the room that was now dark and Grandma finally said, "I thought it was a little bad to fire Floyd that way."

In a while she got up to turn on the light and said, "We have to run up to the church for a minute. The sink's clogged and there's a funeral tomorrow."

Alberta didn't want to go and said she would stay and read but Grandma said she shouldn't stay alone.

Alberta said she did all the time. She hadn't though at night, except for once and that time she had heard a rustling and rustling from the back bedroom and been afraid it was Johnny Rexley. She had tried to go see, telling herself Johnny wasn't mean, just not all there. But she couldn't make herself look and had finally gone to hide in Grandma's house with the lights off so he wouldn't guess that's where she was. She had watched for Mama and Dad's headlights on the lane and had run back before they drove up.

So she put on her shoes and Grandma got her handbag and a broom and dustpan to sweep out the church kitchen while she was there, and they drove to town.

When they got there she wanted to sit in the car and wait. But it was stuffy in the car so she got out and sat on the grass between the church and the parsonage.

There were lights on in the parsonage which was now rented to a teacher since they had no preacher of their own to live there. They had only half a preacher, one shared with the Six Mile Presbyterians and he lived over there. Before him, though, they had a preacher with six kids, including a girl in Alberta's class, Ruthella, a girl who had been in three fifth grade classes and it was only March. She had seen Alberta, the only Methodist, as her best chance and latched onto her for dear life. She would always sit by Alberta and raise her hand to go to the bathroom when Alberta did, and was always demanding that Alberta say whether they were best friends and when Alberta said "I don't know" or "I guess" Ruthella would want to write something down for her to sign. For lunch she ate sandwiches of homemade deer meat sausage, that had a sickening smell. Then all afternoon when Ruthella would come up and want to whisper something you had to smell the sausage again.

She lay on the grass looking at the parsonage lights. Where had that girl gone next with her too-big mouth, always smiling, her eyes always begging like a dog and the wide belt she wore every day because she thought her waist was her best feature. But people got sick of her waist all the time.

Why, since she got so many chances to be new, didn't she try different ways? Why didn't she pretend for example that she had been very popular at the place she had just come from to see if maybe people would believe it? It was such a good chance since Ruthella would be leaving soon anyway and it wouldn't matter too much if didn't work. But maybe some part of it would work, or it would work on a few people and she could do it a little different next time and maybe eventually find a way to act so somebody would like her.

But she couldn't think how Ruthella should act, and she turned to thinking how she and Martha Lee would be airline stewardesses in blue uniforms and little hats, always worrying about whether their stocking seams were straight. In the book about airline stewardesses they were very particular about your stocking seams and one girl who forgot her stockings had to draw the seam up the back of her leg with eyebrow pencil.

Now she wanted to go home and get that book and read more about it before Martha Lee came so she went to try to hurry Grandma up.

She didn't like going into the church when it wasn't Sunday and people weren't there. The long purple windows kept out the light and it was always cold inside even in the hot summer. When she was sitting in there hearing a sermon she always fixed her eyes on one broken pane behind the pulpit, where there was a hole the shape of

India and you could see a piece of sky.

It was not a very big church, not nearly as big as the United Christian, just two rows of wooden pews, a big stove in back and the raised pulpit up front under a picture of a sad young Jesus. Most of the pews were never used, except on Easter and Christmas when all the Laceys came and took every seat. But on an ordinary Sunday, only two rows in the middle of the church were used, where the twelve or so regulars sat, mostly women, huddled together as if to keep warm. Alberta and Mama and Grandma always sat together, Alberta in the middle, Grandma on the right with her Bible in her hand, stiff and watchful that the half-time preacher knew what he was doing. Mama sat on the other side, eyelids drooping. Out of the corner of her eye Alberta would watch Mama's eyelids sinking lower and lower, ready to poke her when her head started to slump.

Dad went sometimes in the winter but usually he was too busy.

And so you looked forward to Christmas and Easter, for the big crowd of Laceys and the refreshments they brought, setting up big shiny coffee makers in the Sunday School room and putting out plates of cookies, making such a nice smell and warmth and of course noise that it didn't seem like church.

The Lacey men came dressed up in suits and neckties, their bellies round and tight in white dress shirts, their faces red and shaven below the white hat line. And one Easter, when Alberta was maybe five, big old Royale Lacey had bowed over her and looking down through his little round glasses said she looked pretty in her Easter dress and shiny black shoes. He asked politely if she would like a cup of tea and she said yes, though she had never had tea before. He brought her a china cup and saucer of tea, half cream with lots of sugar, and had her sit on a chair then put the cup and saucer so she could hold it on her knee. He sat down beside her, a china cup and saucer in his big red hands, a chain running across his huge round belly, and a strange but nice smell coming from him. They had both sipped tea, the most delicious thing she had ever tasted, and suddenly she had known to arch her feet in their patent leather shoes as they rested on the rung of the folding chair, and to smile up at him with her head tipped a little like Mama's. And it hadn't been until that night that she remembered how he had been warmed on their oven door as a tiny baby, his real home in a chicken coop.

Now she went through the main part of the church and into the Sunday School room with its pink flannel boards where the Sunday School teachers could tell Bible stories by sticking figures up on the flannel. It was cold in there too, and crowded with little chairs and tables, with cabinets of old crayons and Sunday School papers and stacked up hymnals and attendance records of children who were probably old and buried by now. There was a little old pump organ with two rows of white knobs that somebody had brought in a covered wagon or maybe just out on an emigrant train. Anyway, it had come from Back East and was too old to throw away now. Sometimes after Sunday School kids tried to make it work but all it would do was puff out stale old air.

Grandma was back in the kitchen, where there was a wood cook stove and an old fashioned sink that you could see the pipes of underneath. Grandma was ramming the plumbers helper down the sink, jamming and jamming it in the glaring light of the one bulb on overhead. It seemed silly that she even bothered to fix the sink. Nobody needed it. Why couldn't they just come put in their hour at church and then go back home where things worked?

"Why bother with it, it'll just get clogged again," she said. She could see the sweat in the criss-cross lines of Grandma's neck.

"There's a funeral here tomorrow and if they use

the kitchen they'll flood water all over everywhere," Grandma said.

"Whose funeral?"

"Some people from Bonner who used to live here."

"Why do they have to have it here?"

Grandma turned angrily.

"Because this is their home church. Their grandparents went here when Papa was alive."

She was in a huff about something so Alberta went back outside. The light from the church windows made an odd purplish glow around her and she sat down to wait for Martha Lee and all the other things to finally start happening.

Soon Grandma came out, carrying the broom and dustpan and patting herself with her handkerchief. She said she wanted to catch her breath before getting into the hot car so she sat down on the steps and Alberta could smell how she had been sweating, the same strong smell as Dad's, but very different from Mama who barely smelled at all. Alberta must take after Mama because when she sniffed her own shirt she couldn't smell anything.

They sat in the purple light, Grandma drying her neck, Alberta stepping on and off planes, either as a stewardess or some kind of rich passenger. But how would she ever get rich?

"If we used to be so rich, why aren't we now?" Alberta asked.

Grandma looked over toward the parsonage as if someone might hear. But they were across a big wide yard.

"Well," she said. "When Papa died bad things happened. Your Uncle Edmund...." she started, and then stopped.

"I just want to know why we aren't still rich," Alberta said. "Not everything that happened."

"Well," Grandma said, "Uncle Edmund was young and of course my mother didn't know anything about the place since Papa handled everything."

"So. Why aren't we still rich?"

"Of course Papa had never made any plans for dying, nobody ever ever expected him to die. He wouldn't even lie down, when he got sick. He sat up in that big old blue chair with his legs up. His legs were all swollen but he would not lie down. He died sitting right there."

Alberta didn't comment, tired of thinking how he might have died.

"After Papa died, Edmund rented the different places out, but the renters didn't run things very well. It didn't seem like we got much money from rent and there were lots of mortgages to pay, more than we knew though of course Papa knew just what it all was. So we needed money and Edmund would take a load of cattle on the train to Omaha to sell."

Grandma paused, looking into the distance.

"Edmund was not a very sensible boy and all the no-goods knew it. They'd hire on to go with him to tend the cattle, then when he'd got the money in Omaha they'd get him to carouse and spend it all."

"At the Crystal Hotel," Alberta said.

"The Crystal Hotel," Grandma said, her voice suddenly coarse. "And one time. One time Alberta, my mother had to borrow money to telegraph it to him at the Crystal Hotel so he and those thieving ruffians could get back home. They'd spent every cent of the cattle money partying and carrying on. And here we were waiting and worrying to death."

Grandma and Alberta both took deep breaths and Grandma patted herself with her handkerchief. Alberta pictured Uncle Edmund, young and scared-eyed, handing out money to a bunch of men who crowded around him in dirty brown hats.

"But it wasn't just the no-goods," Grandma said. "It was everybody in this valley. When a mortgage would come due they would offer to buy cattle for half the price or they would take our hay for a dime on the dollar. They skinned us, they just skinned us to get back at Papa."

"Get back at him for what?" Alberta asked.

"For nothing," Grandma said. "For being better than any of them. And that's how it all slid away, one place after another was foreclosed and to stop it my mother went herself to people who owed Papa money, holding in her hands the notes they'd signed. And they said, 'Why Mrs. Pratt I would do anything to help, but that isn't my note.' Or some would pay but only after the mortgage came due and it was too late. And they knew it Alberta. Don't tell me, don't ever tell me the stinking so-and-so's didn't know it."

Grandma reached her handkerchief to wipe her back, down inside her dress.

"We never asked for a thing," she said. "Except what was rightfully Papa's."

"He should have planned better," Alberta said. "He shouldn't have left you in such a mess."

"He didn't know he was going to die. He was too strong to die, even the doctor said so. He never even laid down."

"Maybe if he'd laid down he would have gotten well," Alberta said.

"So," Grandma said. "It all slipped away. And finally. Finally Alberta they were about to take the home place. Papa's own home place. And we couldn't pay. We didn't have anything."

Grandma's voice shook as Alberta had never heard it do before and it seemed she might even cry.

"Did they?"

"Right then," Grandma said, her voice getting stronger again with anger, "Old Preston Lacey, Royale's father, came down to see Mama. By then the Laceys had their hands on some range land and there were already so many of them they could run cattle all over. It was only people who didn't have anything who ran cattle out on the range. People like Papa had their own land for cattle."

"Except by then his was all gone."

"So Old Preston Lacey came down one night with Royale. He came in and sat in Papa's chair and Royale stood behind, looking at everything. I was just a girl but I wish I'd said, 'Get up out of Papa's chair you old Lacey.'"

Grandma stopped to breathe deeply. Then her voice dropped low and hard as she imitated what Old Man Lacey had said, "'Mrs. Pratt, I'd like to do something for you folks. I'll take over that mortgage and you can pay me back when you get on your feet.'"

Grandma stopped to breathe again.

"When all the time, Alberta. All the time they were thinking there was no way for Mama and me to pay and they'd get the place. Papa's place for them to have and gloat over. To get back at us for having a fine house when they lived in a chicken coop."

They sat a while in the purple light that seemed the color of all the cruel things.

"It was too much," Grandma said, "and Mama died."

Finally Alberta said, "But they didn't get it. Did they?"

"They tried," Grandma said, her voice hard. "But I fooled them. I split with Edmund right then. I took the place with the mortgage and gave him the Sparta property that was left, which of course he lost. Then I married your Grandpa and he worked it and we paid the mortgage to the Laceys every year of his life. I paid it off the year he died. I remember I bought myself a real nightgown because all those years I made my underclothes out of flour sacks. But they never laid a finger on the place, the dirty skunks. And I'll tell you one more thing. Nobody but family is going to lie in Papa's plot."

Grandma's voice cracked. Alberta had never heard her use such strong language as "dirty skunks" and thought maybe she really would cry. Instead she stood up and went back in the church. In a minute the purple glow was gone and Grandma came back out. She locked the church's big front door and after she locked it she yanked on the door to make sure it was tight until the glass in it rattled.

Grandma came back and sat down again, fanning herself with the handkerchief that now itself gave off her strong smell. It was dark except for the lights from the parsonage across the yard and Alberta and Grandma could barely see each other.

After a while Alberta said, "Didn't you ever want to go anywhere? Somewhere far away from here?"

"Yes," Grandma said in the dark. "Once I once wanted to go to China."

"China?"

"Yes. Long ago."

"What gave you the idea of China?"

"A missionary came through who worked in China and I thought I would like to do that too."

Alberta could easily see Grandma in China, wiry and fierce in a strange Chinese sunlight, her sleeves rolled up, grabbing up little Chinese babies to give them some food or a shot or to baptize them, baptizing a long line of them one right after the other.

"Did you try to do it?" Alberta asked.

"I asked our preacher and he had some literature sent," Grandma said.

"That told all about it?"

"It told some."

"Was it exciting?"

"Yes."

In the dark it seemed that maybe they could still have her do it, could go back and re-tell the story with Grandma not staying on the farm and wearing flour sack underwear, not having to get old and fight for whose side of the clothesline it was. Instead, there she would be in China, brave in a pointed Chinese hat. Still fierce and jerky but now out jerking around in China where it was needed, where you did it to survive the diseases and donkey rides and whatever you had to do to get around and save people.

"Well," Alberta said, to keep it a living thing, "what would they have you do?"

"Oh I don't remember," Grandma said. "What they really liked best was husband and wife missionaries. Then I think you went and lived someplace and did practical nursing and taught about cleanliness and so on and then held services and the wife probably led the Bible study and played the piano."

"You could have done all that."

"Oh I expect."

"How old were you when you wanted to?"

"About fourteen."

"So, did you try?"

"Not beyond sending for the literature."

"Why not?" Alberta asked, still feeling there might be some way out of it, some way to have her overcome whatever problems there had been and go. Alberta saw a young Grandma, her hair in smooth black waves down the side of her head, standing up by the store in a straw hat, all her things in two cardboard boxes, tied with string with little rope handles so she could easily carry them both herself. She was standing waiting for the stage to Bonner, going alone but unafraid. Go, Alberta cried back to her. Go and don't even write home for about ten years. Let people here take care of themselves.

"Well," Grandma said, "Papa would never hear of such a thing and of course he was right."

"He was not right. He was not right," Alberta said, raising her voice.

"Hush."

"Why was he right? Why was he the only one who ever got to go away all by himself and do something? Then he left you in a mess."

"He was right," Grandma said, "because my mother was a lady and he wanted me to be a lady...."

"You could have been a lady in China," Alberta

interrupted. "You could have worn a hat and dress and you could have somebody keep sending you stockings."

"Well," Grandma said. "Then he died."

"Good," Alberta said. "The old stinker."

Grandma jumped like lightning and snatched Alberta by the arm, her fingers hard as iron and started smacking Alberta's behind with the straw part of the broom. Alberta twisted away and grabbed the broom and they both held onto it with both hands, Alberta's nose pushed against Grandma's sweaty neck. But Grandma was lots stronger and yanked it away. Alberta ran to the car, jumped in her side and locked the door. Then she thought to lock the other door and lay down in the seat, face down, her feet under the steering wheel.

When Grandma knocked for her to open the door she didn't budge or look up.

Grandma rapped on the window again and said, "Alberta, open this door right now," but she didn't stir, lying on the seat, her hands over her eyes. She blocked Grandma out, picturing how she would go stay with Martha Lee, how they would go to stewardess school together, then fly all over with nothing to worry about but keeping their stocking seams straight. She would never write home and never come back here and she wished Thomas Pratt could look down and see that finally somebody didn't care a thing for him or his farm and would do just what they felt like.

"All right," Grandma said through the door. "I'll just go on uptown to the restaurant and get some pie," and then her steps crunched quickly away.

But she didn't know who she was talking to.

In a few minutes Grandma came back. "Alberta," she said, her voice furious and shaking. "Open that door or I'm going to walk home and wait for your Dad and the company to come."

She waited for a minute, then walked away fast.

She could do it and Alberta listened carefully. But the footsteps stopped after about ten steps. Alberta smiled into her hands since Grandma had ruined her one chance.

She heard Grandma tiptoe back to the church steps, then there was silence. Alberta lay still, knowing that she had won and now it was only a question of how long she wanted it to last.

It would be nice if somebody would come along and see Grandma locked out of the car. Or if it would suddenly get pitch dark.

She thought ahead to when she would finally unlock the door and decided she would not do it until Grandma said she was sorry for hitting her. Alberta knew there were ways to get into a car, since once they had locked the keys in when they had gone to Bonner and had to get a garage man to come and pry open the fly window. But Alberta didn't think Grandma would want to go up to the garage on foot and look silly in front of the greasy garage men. What Grandma was thinking probably was that Alberta would get tired or scared and open the door. But Alberta was lying down comfortably with lots to think about and could stay that way for a long time.

You are under his heel, she said silently, but I'm not.

So they waited, Alberta lying in the car, Grandma sitting on the church step.

After a while Alberta wondered if she could be running out of air and if she could open the window a crack. But that might give Grandma a way to get in. So she put her face lower to the floor instead since surely air leaked in there.

She was almost to doze off in the hot stuffy car when Grandma rapped again on the window, having come up to the car without Alberta hearing.

"Open the door now honey," she said not sounding mad.

Alberta sat up but stared straight ahead in case it was a trick.

"We have to go home now," Grandma said and

after waiting a minute added, "Let's not vex ourselves so."

It seemed that this could be taken as an apology and Alberta was tired of being in the car and not mad anymore. She wanted to go home and read the stewardess book so she unlocked the door.

Grandma got in and they drove home without saying anything and not passing anybody for Grandma to mutter howdedo or bob her head to.

They got to the barnyard and Grandma stopped the car, jerking the hand brake, in a way that made Alberta fear it would come away in her hand.

They sat for a minute and Alberta said, "How did the house burn down?"

Grandma watched through the dark windshield for a while, then said, "Papa set it afire early one morning when he wasn't himself."

"What do you mean he wasn't himself?"

"He wasn't well."

"Was he drunk?"

Grandma held onto the steering wheel and watched through the dark windshield.

After a while, so Alberta could barely hear, she said, "No. Papa never touched liquor."

They got out of the car and smelled the fresh damp night. Behind the houses they could hear the water going by in the ditch.

They walked through the darkness to Grandma's and were going to have a dish of ice cream but Grandma didn't have enough for two dishes. Instead she got out a cellophane package with two chocolate cupcakes and they each had one on a saucer, chocolate on the outside, white goo on the inside. There was enough ice cream to put a little dab on each cupcake. They sat at the table and ate quietly.

Then Grandma got a magazine to read and Alberta went to sleep on the davenport and later, when Mama and Dad came back with Aunt Rae and Martha Lee, they left Alberta in Grandma's, covered with an afghan, to sleep all night and took Martha Lee up over the cellar by herself.

PART FOUR

Martha Lee turned out to be little and soft and boneless with white cat-eye glasses and straight brown hair held back by two round barrettes. That first morning at the breakfast table, amid the fine dishes and crystal, she hung her head and wouldn't speak and even picked her nose once. Whereas when Aunt Rae would address one of her high Southern cries toward Alberta, Alberta would quickly figure out what she had said and give a smart reply.

They sat at breakfast for a long time. Dad put on his boots and went out finally but Mama and Aunt Rae stayed at the table talking. Martha Lee got up and went out on the back porch but then stood just outside the screen door, not knowing where to go.

"Go show Martha Lee around," Mama called to Alberta. Overnight her voice had risen several levels higher in Southern surprise.

Before Alberta got to the door she heard Martha Lee scream as if she'd been murdered. When Alberta got out there she saw it was only Mike jumping up on her, his old tongue hanging out. Martha Lee was turning from side to side screaming with her hands over her face while Mike licked her arms and elbows.

"He just wants you to pet him," Alberta said. "Here Mike, here Mike," and when he jumped up on her, Alberta showed how to pet the back of his bluish neck and make him get down and sit beside you.

Aunt Rae who'd come to the door went back in and Martha Lee said, with her slight Southern accent that she'd kept even in Japan, "I'm scared of dogs."

"That's silly," Alberta said. "They won't hurt you."

"Some will. You should see the attack dogs they had on the base. They were German Shepherds and would bite your throat right out."

"Well," Alberta said. "There are some dogs here that will bite your leg when you ride by on your bicycle or even walk by. And there's a woman who got killed because she was driving along and one of MacIntosh's dogs ran out. She swerved to miss it and ran off the road and broke her neck."

"I thought you said dogs wouldn't hurt you."

"I said Mike wouldn't hurt you."

"You said 'they' wouldn't hurt you."

"I meant dogs like Mike."

"Ha," Martha Lee said. "You're changing your tune."

"I am not changing my tune."

She patted old Mike's neck, then acted like she was hunting for something in his fur. Mike sat still, his big tongue out panting.

"What's that?" Martha Lee said finally, pointing across the barnyard.

"You mean the barn?" Alberta asked warily, since she thought everybody would know what a barn was.

"That thing hanging out of the top."

Alberta looked up where Martha Lee was pointing and saw a round gray thing hooked to ropes hanging from a pole at the top of the barn. She'd never noticed it before and didn't have any idea what it was.

"That's to scare off pigeons," she said. "But it doesn't work."

"Pigeons fly in there?"

"Oh yeah lots. They get manure all over everything. They get it all over the jeep I drive sometimes when I can get a push. I drive all over."

Martha Lee said, "I found a little tiny bottle of wine in the airport. I have it in my suitcase right upstairs."

"Like fun," Alberta said.

"I do," Martha Lee said. "It's real cute. It's in a little straw cover."

Alberta believed Martha Lee did have a little straw-covered bottle of wine and wanted more than anything to see it. She said, "It probably isn't really wine. It's probably grape juice."

When Martha Lee didn't reply, Alberta said, "Anyway, where is it?"

"It's in my bedroom," Martha Lee said, apparently meaning up over the cellar. So they went up there, where the red and white crepe paper looked kind of nice, drooping over the messed up bed and Martha Lee's suitcase, which was sitting open spilling things out onto the floor. Attached to the inside of the suitcase were little pouches of pleated silky material. The little pouches nearly broke Alberta's heart as she imagined how it would be to gather up your own things out of the bathroom and bedroom and put them into little pockets as you prepared to go traveling.

Martha Lee rummaged in the suitcase, looking first in one half, then the other. It was so funny to have a strange girl here rummaging in a suitcase that Alberta looked toward the door, almost expecting that she would also see Buford standing there in his red shirt with the two rows of white buttons, smoking his little yellow cigarette.

"I've only lost one thing all this time," Martha Lee said, in her Southern accent. "I lost a hairbrush on Guam," to which Alberta couldn't think of a reply.

Finally Martha Lee pulled out a paper sack wrapped with string and tied in a dozen knots.

"Is that it?" Alberta asked.

"Yes," Martha Lee said, and squatted down to untie it.

"Don't open it here. We better go out to my fort."

So they climbed back down the ladder, Martha Lee hiding the paper sack under her shirt.

They went across the road and Alberta showed Martha Lee how to get through the fence, holding one wire up and one wire down so you could make a hole big enough to climb through. After they got through Martha Lee stopped and looked all around and said, "Are there any animals in here?"

"Not now," Alberta said. "They took all the cattle to the hills."

"Where are the hills?"

"A long ways away."

"Are you positive they all went."

"Yes. I walk though here all the time. There's some duck decoys but they aren't real. If you see ducks, don't worry."

So they walked across the field, Alberta walking fast and Martha Lee having to pant to keep up. She was funny looking, so little and soft in her green pedal pushers and little white shirt with the tail that was too short to stay tucked in. She seemed kind of goofy behind the white glasses and it was hard to imagine she was a year older and had traveled everywhere.

Alberta told about things as they walked across the field. She told about hot wire fences that would give you a shock and how you could tell whether a fence was hot or not by looking for the white glass insulators, kind of like a spool of thread, that held the wire away from the fence post. If you saw that, you should assume the fence was hot and not touch it, even though it might not be turned on. You should never, never touch it if you were standing in a ditch. And she told about the little boy she'd heard of who grabbed a hot wire fence when he was standing in a ditch and couldn't let go and his father had to come and pull him off.

"Did he die?" Martha Lee asked.

"No. But electricity went through his whole body for about five minutes."

She pointed out the baling twine and showed how the Laceys would pop it off a bale of hay, shaking out the hay to the cattle then tossing the twine away. She told how the Laceys were short and merry with fat faces and ear muffs under their cowboy hats and she imitated them staggering around on the hay wagon. She told how they would call out to her as she was walking across the field. She told what she yelled back to them, making up several funny things. She felt she should add, "The Laceys act nice now but they tried to steal our place once."

"What place?"

"Our farm. Our barn and house and fields."

"How can you steal a farm?" Martha Lee asked. "Everybody would know you had it."

"Well, they tried to get it away from us and live on it themselves I guess."

Alberta pointed out the duck decoys which made Martha Lee stop in her tracks. She wouldn't keep going until Alberta went over and threw one up and let it thud back to the ground to convince her they were just wood.

They went on and soon could see the fort, its yellow curtain hanging nicely between the two trees.

When she saw it Martha Lee said, "Oh cute."

"Oh," Alberta said. "It's just an old fort."

They went in and sat down on the baling twine couch.

Martha Lee started trying to undo the wine and spent a long time untying all the knots before she finally got down to the sack. She unwrapped it and pulled out a green bottle, kind of like a small ketchup bottle with a little straw case that went all around the bottom of the bottle. On the label it said, "Chianti."

"What's Chianti?" Alberta asked.

"It's another word for wine," Martha Lee said.

"Where did you find it?"

"In the ladies' room in San Francisco. Laying right by the sink. I saw the lady who lost it too. She came back in and hunted all around but I had it in my purse. I kept washing my hands all the time she hunted."

"What was she like?" Alberta asked.

"She had diamond rings on both hands. She had black hair, crimped real tight to her head and a black fur coat."

The woman sounded made up and if she was real Alberta still could not imagine taking and hiding her bottle of wine and then washing your hands brazenly while she hunted for it.

"Our neighbor is a drinker," Alberta said, to top this story. "He drives to Bonner every day at three to get a bottle of whiskey. He gets a bottle three times as big as this."

Martha Lee was still struggling to get the cork out of the bottle.

After a second Alberta added, "Sometimes he goes crazy and takes off all his clothes."

"Did you ever see him with his clothes off?" Martha Lee asked.

"No," Alberta said finally. "Maybe it isn't true."

Martha Lee pulled the cork with her fingers, then her teeth. When she finally got it out she said, "OK, let's drink some."

"Drink some wine?"

"Yeah. Smell."

Alberta took a whiff of the bottle and jerked back. The smell was teeming, evil and sickening, much worse than silage or the faint smell of liquor that rose up around the pool hall.

"You have to hold your breath," Martha Lee said.

"Have you already drunk some?"

"No."

But now Martha Lee put the bottle to her lips and turned it up and drank. Alberta could tell by the surprised look in her eyes that she had really drunk.

Alberta didn't have any idea what might happen.

"You'd better try to throw up," she said.

"No," Martha Lee said. "It's OK. Just don't take such a big drink."

"I'm not going to drink any."

"Why not?"

"Because. We don't believe in it. We never touch liquor."

"Do you believe in God?" Martha Lee said. "I don't."

Alberta was shocked that the wine could take effect so fast. She thanked heaven she hadn't tasted it or even smelled it more than once.

"Come on," she said, getting up. "We have to go back."

Martha Lee put the cork back in the bottle. She went out of the fort but lay down again on the grass, her little white glasses reflecting the sunlight. She still had the straw-covered bottle in her hand.

"I don't believe in you," she yelled up to the sky.

"Quit it," Alberta said. "You can talk that way at your own place but not here."

She tugged on Martha Lee's little arm, trying to pull her up but Martha Lee had gone limp as a dead chicken. Alberta looked around to see if anybody could possibly see them, partly afraid there might be, partly wishing somebody would come help.

"Let's play wild stallions," Martha Lee said.

She got up on her hands and knees, then started kicking up her feet, snorting and trying to whinny.

"Come on," she said. "You be one too."

But it looked babyish and Alberta didn't want to. She couldn't see how Martha Lee could turn straight from not believing in God to playing horses. She couldn't see how someone could be afraid of ducks and drooling old dogs, and then dare to lie on their back under the open sky and yell at God.

"I'm a stallion, I'm a stallion," Martha Lee yelled, still snorting and kicking up her heels in a stupid way. Alberta wanted to get away but couldn't go and leave her own cousin drunk and so far from home. Finally she sat down on the grass a little ways off.

"I know where there might be some human bones buried," she said.

Martha Lee stopped kicking her feet around and crawled over to sit by Alberta panting.

"Whose bones?"

"An old sheepherder they might have murdered a long time ago."

"How do you know?"

"My uncle told me. It might just be a story though.

Half the stuff he says he makes up."

"Why did they murder him?"

"Oh, everything was kind of rough in those days. If you were a lady you had to be careful that something didn't happen."

"What?"

"I don't know. Just I guess, people drinking and cussing and everything."

Alberta trailed off, embarrassed since Martha Lee had herself just been drinking and in a way cussing.

"Let's dig up the bones," Martha Lee said.

"OK," Alberta said, glad to have her off God. "It's not certain. But if there are and we found them they might hold a trial and we could testify."

"We could get in the newspaper," Martha Lee said. "They would take our picture holding the shovel."

"We could get in the newspaper anyway. You just call up Edna and tell her any news about yourself and she puts it in. Mrs. Elmore Jones calls and gets in every week. And she doesn't do anything. 'Mrs. Elmore Jones motored to Bonner.' 'Mrs. Leonard Jones had a visit from her sister.' 'Mrs. Elmore Jones was home with the flu all last week.'"

"They'll put in anything?"

"Yeah. It's because Edna gets paid for how much she puts in. I was in one time for figuring out the population."

"Let's do," Martha Lee said. "Let's call up and give her a story about ourselves. Even if we don't find the bones."

"OK. I don't know if she would take it from kids though."

"We could write it. I can copy my mother's handwriting so nobody can tell. I do it all the time. I sign my own notes."

"If it was too crazy she wouldn't put it in," Alberta said. "She would know it wasn't something from around here."

"It won't be too crazy."

"OK," Alberta said, relieved that the drunkenness seemed to be wearing off. Pretty soon they got up and started to walk back across Laceys' field, after first hiding the bottle of wine under a log a ways from the fort so no one finding it would think it was theirs.

When they got close to the house Alberta said, "You better not tell anybody you drank that wine."

"I won't."

"I might drink later on, I don't know," Alberta said.

"There's lots left."

"I mean when I'm older. I might try it anyway."

"How old are you?"

"Eleven. But I don't think twelve is old enough either."

"Yeah," Martha Lee said. "It makes you feel sick." Which made it seem like she probably took back what she'd said about God too.

By the time Martha Lee had been there a week they had done nearly everything. They had ridden the bicycle up to the old livery stable with an irrigation shovel they had secretly borrowed from Grandma. But after a few inches of softness, the ground by the livery stable turned into near rock and they couldn't keep digging.

They had ridden all though town and the trailer court and one supper time acted like they were fixing their bike tire across the road from the Robinses to try and see how many people went in the trailer at once. But while they saw four or five different Robinses, there was no general time of coming or going and they never got to see eight or nine people cram in at once.

They had gone up in the barn, but Martha Lee was more interested in the milking parlor than the old things in the loft, and would go every evening to crouch in the far corner as the two big old milk cows came lumbering over the step, their bags swaying heavily from side to side, their blundering hooves echoing on the wood plank floor. She kept being afraid of them, even though Alberta explained and explained that a milk cow was the last thing to be afraid of, that they just walked around in a stupid daze and they weren't smart enough to think of hurting you.

"Look in their eyes," she had told Martha Lee. "See how stupid they are?"

Still Martha Lee was afraid and would squeak every time one of them stumbled or lurched coming into the barn, as if it was their very living bigness that scared her. She would sit in the far corner watching while Dad milked, and wouldn't ever go milk herself as Alberta did sometimes to see how it felt. Alberta urged Martha Lee to do it. It was strange and creepy to pull on the long freckled teats, the skin slipping up and down. You had to squeeze hard or nothing came out but you could barely force yourself to do it. Also the cows would switch their tails in your face and sometimes drop big plops of manure so you had to snatch the bucket up out of the way. But none of that made it scary, only something you didn't want to do more than once or twice.

Alberta had tried to have Martha Lee ride their gentlest horse, Copper, saddling him up while Martha Lee sat high on the fence, making a squawk every time Copper shifted his feet. Alberta had thought when Martha Lee saw how gentle Copper was she would get on and at least ride around the barnyard where there were no ditches or anything to stumble over, and Alberta had ridden back and forth in the barnyard, with no hands and even sitting backwards to show how safe it was. She urged and urged Martha Lee to do it, promising nothing bad would happen and that Martha Lee would like it. But Martha Lee didn't dare, and Alberta puzzled over what it was that made Martha Lee afraid of things and what didn't.

One afternoon they went over to Rexleys' to see the tropical fish and Ione's dolls and Old Man Rexley in his chair. Another fish had turned up missing and now there were only two, a pink one and one of see-through green.

"I can't imagine what went with it," Ione said. "It was that white fan-shaped one. I'm going wild trying to figure it out."

They sat on the couch and ate macaroons while Ione talked and embroidered more green bathroom curtains.

"How come your former husband never came back the last time?" Martha Lee asked after they had been there a while and heard all Ione's regular stories. Alberta blushed at such a question, but Ione didn't seem to mind.

"I'll tell you what I think," Ione said. "And people can laugh all they want."

She put down her embroidery to change a pin in her high black hair-do. Alberta and Martha Lee frowned seriously.

"He loved me better than anybody else," Ione said. "And that's why he kept coming back for three years. But he was a traveling man and I think it finally got the best of him."

Ione finished with her hair and raised her chin to look down the room at Old Man Rexley.

"How come you didn't get a job and stay so you could try to find somebody else?" Martha Lee asked.

"I'll tell you, Martha Lee," Ione said. "I went to Portland when I was seventeen, and got a job and met my husband. Well, that was all the get-up-and-go I had in me. And anyway I didn't have the feet to keep waitressing."

They looked down at her heavy feet in brown oxfords.

"It's in the arch," Ione said. "So I came back to take care of Dad. But now he can't last much longer."

With Martha Lee there, every minute was tight and floating as a balloon and Alberta didn't want to waste any of it on a party for the Sunday School kids and so forgot the whole idea. But the first Saturday of the visit Mama had her barbecue in the side yard. She set up a long table with yellow roses and oil lanterns and Aunt Rae made pink paper shades to give the lamps a magic glow in a way that had never been seen in Oregon before.

Three couples came and sat telling stories until long after dark. They sat in the lantern light, laughing and laughing, lifted and carried by the high Southern cries until it seemed the farm had floated into a pink Alabama sunset.

Alberta didn't want to leave for a second but when she and Martha Lee went in to bring out dessert they saw Grandma, who wasn't invited, standing behind the house listening.

"Oh, hello girls," Grandma said. "I thought I smelled smoke."

In the second week they began spying on Old Man Rexley, going every day after dinner to crouch in the dark corn and watch for him to come through the weeds to pour from his bottle into the ditch.

Alberta told how he claimed he was just rinsing his bottle, but Martha Lee said, "It's whiskey. My daddy has whiskey and it's just that color."

"Do you think we should tell?" Alberta asked. "I wonder if it hurts the corn."

But they didn't tell and kept hiding back in the shady corn jungle to watch him come every day in his rubber boots, wading through the high weeds on the ditch bank, then squatting and pouring, sometimes taking off his old brown hat and scratching his head, that, surprisingly, had lots of hair like a boy's, though white. Finally he would turn and go and in a minute they would hear his pickup start with a roar for the trip to Bonner.

One day he interrupted himself in the middle of scratching his head and stepped across the ditch and into the corn to grab each of them by the neck before they could get up and run. He hauled them both out of the corn and held them both by the collar.

"Now then," he said. "I guess I have to call the sheriff."

"Why?" Alberta said finally.

"Why? I guess they haven't made spying legal yet. Do you know what they used to do to spies? Say!"

He shook them once and then let them go to stand in front of him.

"Shot them," Martha Lee said. "But that was spying for an enemy. It wasn't just watching somebody."

"Yeah," Alberta said. "And this is our cornfield."

Old Man Rexley stood looking down at them and Martha Lee finally said, "We just thought it was funny you kept pouring your whiskey out and then driving to get more."

"Who else thinks its funny?"

"Nobody," Alberta said. "We haven't told anybody. Yet."

Old Man Rexley took off his hat and sat down on the ditch bank. He ran his hand through his thick white hair.

"Now," Old Man Rexley said, changing his tone. "You are two nice little girls. So I think you can understand something."

Alberta and Martha Lee kept quiet, moving outside his reach.

"Now here's the deal," Old Man Rexley started, then he stopped.

"I don't get the chance to talk to anybody much," he said. "And I'm rusty. Wait a minute while I stop and think."

They stood on the ditch bank watching him.

"Now," he said in a minute. "Here's the deal. Back twenty years ago sure I'd take a drink. Back in the thirties everybody drank. After they dried it up people went to drinking that never took a drink in their lives. Do you know Horace Decker that still lives up in town?"

"That's the one that always yells he doesn't want a

magazine subscription," Alberta told Martha Lee.

"Now he had a keg in his cellar and a hose that came out through a hole in the back of the house. You'd give him two bits and then go around back and suck on the hose until you'd had two bits worth. Then he'd crimp the hose off."

Old Man Rexley ran his hand through his hair as if thinking.

"God they drank a lot of whiskey in those days," he said. "I remember one time, when I was riding for Laceys. We found a ten gallon keg. We cracked it open and all got drunk and went to tearing around. We rode through a sheepherder's camp and trampled his stove and tent. Not meaning to, but Old Man Lacey, Royale's dad, made us pay for it out of our wages anyway. Then the fella that lost the whiskey found out about it and he started to beller and yell. So Old Man Lacey made us pay him back too. We was paying on that one drunk for six months."

"So then you couldn't stop drinking once you'd started?" Alberta asked.

"No," Old Man Rexley said. "I could always take it or leave it. I quit riding for Laceys and got married and went to farming right here. We didn't have any money, we bought all our grub with eggs, what we couldn't raise. Everything simple. Nowdays everybody wants money so they can get their grub from a package. Now they got to have storebought hairdos and a bowl of fish. But then we didn't care so much about money. Eggs was good enough for us."

Old Man Rexley hawked and spit in the ditch.

"I'd like to see this country back like it was," he said. "A man knows a fresh egg."

They stood on the ditch bank, waiting to see if he was going to tell them why he was pouring out the whiskey or if he'd jumped the track.

"Now then," he said. "Ione is just biding her time, waiting for me to die. Waiting for her puke-colored bathroom, excuse me ladies. Isn't that true?"

"Yes," Alberta said.

"Do you think that's right? Say!"

"No," Alberta said. "Not if you can still talk and everything."

"Wellsir, she started waiting for me to die a long time before I stopped talking. She come back from California after that gigolo run off. She come back and her feeling was, 'If you could just die I could sell this house and farm Johnny out somewhere and get on back to my gigolo hunting.'"

"What's a gigolo?" Alberta asked.

"Somebody who marries you and then runs off," Martha Lee said.

"That's right," Old Man Rexley said. "And there aren't many around. You'll find one thing and another but it's hard to fine a real honest-to-goodness professional gigolo and it's the only thing Ione ever figured out to do in her life. Went clear to Portland to get him. Just think how she had to hunt and beat the bushes and knock herself out until she finally found one."

"How do you know he was a gigolo?" Alberta asked. "Maybe something happened to him."

"Ha. I knew something was funny about him when I saw him. Too good-looking for one thing in that greasy kind of way. Looked me right in the eye, as much as to say, 'I'm a gigolo and your daughter came and scared me up and so now I'm gonna do what I have to do, I guess you understand that.' And I looked him right back as if to say, 'Oh sure, I understand fine. I understand the whole dang thing, don't trouble yourself.'

"When she run off to Portland I says to her, 'You're leaving, but you'll be back.' She says, 'I'm never coming back.' But then she did come back to show off what she'd scared up. 'Eugene's been in all forty-eight states,' she told me.

"I says, 'What's he been doing in all those forty-eight states, I wonder.'

"She says, 'Selling shoes.'"

"Didn't he sell shoes?" Alberta asked. "In a blue Studebaker?"

"I don't know if he sold shoes," Old Man Rexley said. "It ain't the point."

"Maybe he got killed in a wreck and his body went over a cliff and was never found," Martha Lee said.

"Maybe," Old Man Rexley said. "But it came to life long enough to draw all the money out of the bank so that when Ione paid the rent the next time her check bounced."

"Well," Alberta said. "I don't blame her if she wants to go back to California. People don't have to stay here forever."

"Heck no. Let her go. Let her go chasing the bright lights. But I'm not gonna sit still while she kills me off and takes everything I ever done in this valley and trades it in for a gigolo. And that's why I come down here and pour out a bottle of whiskey every day that she thinks I'm drinking. And you little girls are on your honor not to tell. Because you said yourself, it isn't right."

"She thinks you're drinking yourself to death but you aren't?" Martha Lee guessed.

"That's right. I ain't. I'll bury her and still have my place, and soon as she's gone I'll put in a flush toilet. And I'll get one of those furry covers for the toilet seat."

"Maybe if she didn't think you were going to die pretty soon she would give up and leave anyway," Alberta said. "Even without any money. She could probably get a job in a dime store or something."

"Maybe she would," Old Man Rexley said. "But I don't want her to leave. I want her to stay here and haul her rear end out to that privy for twenty more winters, excuse me ladies, and sit there in the flies twenty more summers. Since she's so anxious to get away from here. Since she's so anxious to trade me in for a gigolo."

"Well," Alberta said. "I think it's a dirty trick."

"Oh?" Old Man Rexley said, pushing his hat back on his head so he could stare at her. "Is that so? Maybe you're another one of them."

Alberta and Martha Lee began edging down the ditch bank, in case he should start chasing them.

"Oh now," Old Man Rexley said. "I know you are nice little girls and here's the deal. Looky." He reached in his pocket and brought out a green bill and held it up in front of him. "See this ten dollar bill. Here's what I'm gonna do. I'm gonna tear it right in two, see here?" As he spoke he took the ten dollar bill and gently ripped it up the middle. "Now then," he said. "I'm going to give one half of it to you little girls and keep the other half. And if you don't tell anybody I'll give it to you."

"When?" Martha Lee asked.

"Oh pretty soon."

"I'm leaving in a week," Martha Lee said.

"All right at the end of a week then," Old Man Rexley said. "Next Monday morning you come down here and I'll give you the other half. If you don't say nothing."

Alberta and Martha Lee looked at each other for a minute and then Martha Lee went over to get the ten dollar half. Old Man Rexley reached down to shake her hand and then stretched out his hand to Alberta so she went to shake it too.

"There now," Old Man Rexley said, tucking away his half of the bill. "Reasonable people can always make a deal." He waded back through the weeds on the ditch bank.

They were in on Grandma's floor cutting out matching shirts from some flowered percale when Adelaide came unexpectedly for a visit, driving up alone. She hurried across the front lawn, grinning and winking as she came and patting Mike who jumped up on her.

"What's she coming for?" Alberta asked but Grandma didn't answer.

"Who is it?" Martha Lee asked as they watched Adelaide cross the lawn.

"Uncle Edmund's wife. She wants to get buried in our cemetery plot."

"Why hello Adelaide," Grandma said nicely as she got to the door and when she was sat down Grandma went to make tea. Adelaide chatted with Alberta and Martha Lee, complimenting them on their shirts and saying how she could tell they had gotten to be practically twins anyway.

When the tea came, Adelaide kept chatting away, telling things from her church in Bonner where she said they had had a fire in the church kitchen.

"Law," Grandma said. "How did that happen?"

"Well," Adelaide said, winking at Alberta and Martha Lee. "The youth group was having an Old Testament party. They all came in their bathrobes and pasted cotton on their faces for beards."

"Who ever heard of such a thing," Grandma said.

Adelaide nodded her head as if to agree.

"That woman preacher has some new ideas," she said.

"What did they eat?" Martha Lee asked.

Adelaide said, "I'm not sure what all they ate."

"Angel food cake?" Martha Lee guessed.

"Maybe that was it," Adelaide said.

"How did the fire start?" Alberta asked.

"Well they'd had their program, as I heard it, and some of the young people had already gone. The ones left behind started a fire to burn the trash from their supper and somebody had brought a ouija board and they started to ask it things."

"A what?" Grandma said.

"A ouija board," Martha Lee said. "You put your fingers on a pointer and ask it questions and spirits answer you. You can ask like, 'Who will I marry,' and it will spell out a name."

"Have you ever done it?" Alberta asked.

"Once," Martha Lee said.

"What did you ask it?"

"Who I would marry."

"What did it say?"

"Ut."

"Ut?"

"U.T. It could be his initials."

"They have these kind of goings-on in a Methodist church?" Grandma said. "Why don't they start up a poker game I wonder or go down to the pool hall?"

"How'd the fire get started?" Alberta asked.

"Well as I heard it, they started asking the board religious questions."

"Law," Grandma said.

Adelaide looked down sadly as if to agree but went on. "They asked it to tell when Jesus would come back. But it started spelling out 'D. E. V.' like it was going to spell devil. They got so scared they threw the whole board in the stove, and it flared up and started a fire in the chimney. They all ran out but the man from next door saw the smoke and put it out with his garden hose."

"What is this world coming to," Grandma said.

Adelaide just shook her head and looked down sadly, peeking up once to wink at Alberta and Martha Lee.

"Oh," Adelaide said in a minute, as if the thought had just come to mind. "I have Edmund's and my stone with me."

Grandma stared out at the west window to the mountains and didn't reply. Adelaide said, "I brought it out to show you how they inscribed it. It's in the trunk."

Grandma didn't reply. Adelaide looked straight at her and asked, "Would you like to see it, Lucille?"

"No thank you, Adelaide," Grandma said, her mouth a little line and her tea cup jiggling slightly in its saucer.

"Well," Adelaide said. "It's right out in the trunk."

"How heavy is it?" Martha Lee asked.

"It weighs a ton," Adelaide said, winking.

The stone was probably too heavy for Adelaide and Uncle Edmund to even lift out of their trunk. Alberta felt sorry for them, having to carry it around forever unless Grandma let them put it in the cemetery.

"It will keep you on the road in the snow if you still have it this winter," Alberta said.

"There's a lot of space down there Lucille," Adelaide said. "In your area."

Grandma held her lips together and looked out the west window where you could see the row of Indians marching in the afternoon sunlight.

"I expect two more won't make much difference," Adelaide said, smiling.

Grandma finally said, "Things can go fast once they start."

"Forgive us our trespasses," Adelaide said, her voice still bright. "As we forgive those who trespass against us."

But Grandma drew up stiff, watching out the window.

"He was only a boy," Adelaide said.

"Who?" Martha Lee asked.

"Uncle Edmund," Alberta said. "When he lost our property."

"That's right," Grandma said. "And he's not giving away any more of it. Not even six feet."

They could hear her breathing and smell her strong smell.

Finally Adelaide said Well, she hated to rush off but she had be getting back because she never liked to drive that Bonner road after dark, the way the logging trucks whizzed around the curves.

Still she sat, as if waiting, but Grandma didn't speak. Eventually she got up and left. They watched her hurry across the lawn, one side of her old skinny bottom higher than the other.

After she was gone Grandma went and took a sponge bath to get ready to go down to the cemetery and make sure nobody had bothered anything and that somebody hadn't by chance already dug a spot for a double stone.

They all three got in Grandma's car and drove down to the cemetery and walked over to their plot.

When they got to their corner of the cemetery, they found everything just like it had always been with only the same old tombstones for Grandma's mother, father and husband with lots of grassy space all around them. Nobody had been digging to put in a new stone.

Grandma wanted to pull a few weeds around the stones while she was down there and rake up leaves, and Martha Lee wanted to explore. It was getting a little dark to be wandering through the cemetery, but Alberta went, walking between the rows of graves. Martha Lee though walked right over the tops of the graves.

"How would you like it if somebody walked over your grave?" Alberta asked.

"Fine," Martha Lee said. "I would be glad they did and gave me some company."

"You wouldn't be alive to be glad of anything."

"I know. So what difference does it make?"

She kept doing it and Alberta kept walking in between because she didn't think it was respectful, it didn't matter whether the dead people knew it or not.

They read some of the names and looked at the interesting tombstones, the one that was a kind of tin steeple where they used to hide bootleg whiskey and the ones with little white lambs to show where babies were buried. They looked at a tall tombstone for Mrs. Ira Felty which had a photograph of a stiff lady in high collar and glasses on a chain. Under the photograph it read, "Too good for this Life."

Martha Lee pretended to be Mrs. Ira Felty with her nose in the air, too good for everything until she dropped dead of it. She fell down on Mrs. Ira Felty's grave, lying spraddled out over the hump.

"Get up," Alberta said, goose bumps popping out all over her.

Martha Lee wanted to tell ghost stories but Alberta wouldn't, not in the cemetery but said she would if they went and got in the car. When they were there Martha Lee told a story about three Japanese girls who climbed up a misty mountain and met three ghosts who scared them nearly to death but it turned out the ghosts only wanted to tell their fortunes, each ghost being assigned to tend the fortune of each girl. One girl had a bad fortune while the other two had good fortunes. But on the way down the mountain the girl with the bad fortune killed the other two.

"So the good fortunes didn't come true?" Alberta asked.

"No," Martha Lee said. "The girl with the bad fortune got rich and married a prince and lived happily every after."

"What's it mean?" Alberta asked.

"It doesn't mean anything," Martha Lee said. "That's just what happened."

"Ha," Alberta said. "It means something. You just don't know what."

The only story Alberta could think of at the moment was the one about the killer whose hook was found on the car door but she didn't want to tell that sitting in a car by the cemetery. She didn't want Martha Lee to know about the papooses or the Chinese they drowned.

Finally Grandma came and they drove back home, Grandma muttering and saying "Howdedo" to Ione Rexley who was out in her yard singeing a chicken with a roll of burning newspaper.

"Do you think Old Man Rexley will drink himself to death pretty soon?" Martha Lee asked and they both watched Grandma closely.

"Oh," Grandma said. "That old stinker won't die until he can cause trouble by it."

Before Martha Lee left, they went over to Rexleys' once more to look at Old Man Rexley now that they knew he was pretending.

"He's drunk himself into his second childhood," Ione said. "What do you think I caught him doing?"

Alberta and Martha Lee said they didn't know.

"Trying to drink out of my fish bowl."

They all looked down the room at Old Man Rexley but he didn't twitch a muscle and his little cigarette drooped down dead.

The day before Martha Lee had to leave they went down to the ditch to wait for Old Man Rexley but he never came.

"He's tricking us," Alberta said. "All right, we'll tell."

But Martha Lee thought he'd just forgotten and Alberta should keep trying to get the other half. Then she could tape it together, change it for two five dollar bills, and send Martha Lee one.

When it was time for Martha Lee to go, Alberta wouldn't leave the room up over the cellar but stayed stretched across the bed in her matching shirt crying. Martha Lee cried too but had to stop and go get her hair put up for the trip. Finally Alberta stopped crying and lay on the bed like a big empty sack, not knowing how she could bear to start making everything up by herself again.

In a while Martha Lee came back up with a news item to send to Edna for the paper. It was written in a grown-up looking hand on Aunt Rae's blue stationery. It said, "Mrs. Ira Felty of Boise was in the valley over the weekend visiting friends. She motored back to Boise on Monday."

Then Martha Lee and Aunt Rae got in the car to drive to the airport and Alberta went in to Grandma's where they silently each had a store-bought cupcake.

As soon as Aunt Rae sent an address where they were in Alabama, Alberta mailed Martha Lee a ten-page letter about all they would do when they lived someplace such as France together. She also sent the clipping from the newspaper about Mrs. Ira Felty. It would give Martha Lee a big kick because it appeared at the top of the column and got the headline, "Valley Visitors Welcomed."

Alberta didn't mention the other half of the ten dollars which she hadn't been able to collect, though she had waited at the ditch several times.

In a couple of weeks another item came for Alberta to send in saying, "Mrs. Ira Felty received visitors from Alabama last week."

Martha Lee enclosed a letter saying she had a sore place on her chest that was the start of her bosom. But she wondered why there was only one. She and her friend Suzanne were both saving up to get some boy's Levis which was what all the girls there wore.

Then there was a long pause. They started corn cutting and fed men at dinner again every day in the tired heat of September. Dad told how crazy he'd flown during the war and after dinner Mama went behind the chicken house to lie in the sun, her eyes covered with tin foil circles. Alberta, looking down at her, could see that her secrets, if she had any, weren't going to get her anywhere.

The last week of corn cutting Grandma got in a wreck up by the store when the sun was in her eyes and she ran into a horse trailer. It didn't hurt her but it jolted her and broke her glasses. Without them she couldn't see, but two young Laceys, Oliver and Dennis, who were just coming out of the store, helped her go sit down in the shade for a minute to calm down. Then one drove her home in their pickup, the other one driving her car. They walked her up to the house holding her arm and treated her so nice that she wouldn't yet even mention it.

Alberta went across Laceys' field to find the bottle of wine and smash it on a rock so she wouldn't be tempted to drink it some day.

Toward the end of corn cutting another news item finally came. It read, "Friends received word that Mrs. Ira Felty of Boise had fallen and broken her back. She is hospitalized but may not get better."

This item too got the headline, "Tragedy Suffered," which Alberta sent to Martha Lee the next day. But it wasn't until after Halloween that another item came. It said, "Friends were grieved to hear that Mrs. Ira Felty of Boise has passed away."

Alberta sent it in to Edna and the next week mailed the item, which fell behind "United Christian Cake Sale Set," to Martha Lee with a letter suggesting that they both try to become exchange students to France in a year or two. But Martha Lee never replied.

On the cold fall nights, listening to the radio, Alberta practiced copying Martha Lee's grownup handwriting and the day after Thanksgiving sent an anonymous letter to Ione Rexley. It read, "Please come back to California. I am still alive and trying to find you. Your Eugene."